# Rainie Err

Book Five of the Rainie Series

Melody Muckenfuss

Copyright © 2013 by Melody Muckenfuss
Cover photography by Melody Muckenfuss

All rights reserved

This book, or parts thereof, may not be reproduced in any form without permission of the author

For information: melodymuck@gmail.com
www.melodymuckenfuss.com

BOOKS BY MELODY MUCKENFUSS

**The Rainie Series**

Rainie Daze
Rainie Knights
Rainie Missed
Rainie Whether

**The Red Wolf Series**
(Mel Kindley)

Rise of the Red Wolves
Howl of the Red Wolves
Hunt for the Red Wolves

**The Shadow Series**
(Mel Kindley)

Shadow

Find all of Melody's books at:
**www.melodymuckenfuss.com**
**www.facebook.com/rainieseries**

This one is for Bobby, a true friend in the past, present, and all the futures that may come.

# Chapter One

It was unseasonably warm for late April, easily seventy-five degrees and not a cloud in the blue sky, and I was taking full advantage of it. Michigan winters sometimes tend to linger, bringing snow down to cover the daffodils all the way into May.

Not this year. The last snow had been weeks ago, and although I was well aware that we weren't completely safe from the white stuff, there was a pretty good chance that spring was here to stay.

It was Monday, and I had decided to treat myself to a day off. Last week had been pretty stressful. I had gotten between a couple of bad guys and their stolen money, and one of them had held a gun to Thelma's head and insisted I give him the money.

Thelma is my best friend, but she is also, technically, a client. I provide home care for the elderly - among other career choices - and Thelma had hired me to be her companion, mostly because she thought it was amusing at the time. The truth is she is less in need of a caregiver than I am; in fact, when I raced in to rescue her, she pretty much managed to handle the problem herself.

Today I was trying to put all of that out of my head. Normally I work Monday mornings, taking care of a stubborn but lovable woman named Maggie, who hadn't wanted me in her life at all. She was slowly warming up to me, but today she was off to Chicago on a shopping expedition with her daughter.

I was sitting in my backyard with a notebook on my lap, working on a little poetry. George, my pet iguana, was sunning himself on a low tree branch. I had fastened a nylon harness around his shoulders and I had a firm grip on the end of his leash. He wasn't much for being walked like a dog, but he did like natural sunlight. He was getting ready to shed his skin, so he was a bit cranky. I thought this little treat might improve his mood. I wasn't sure if it was working or not. Being a reptile, he doesn't say much, so I had to pretty much judge by whether or not he chose to whip me with his tail when I approached him.

I leaned my head against the back of my lawn chair and closed my eyes, hoping the heat of the sun on my face would ignite my muse. It had been some time since I'd written anything.

There was a wren singing its little heart out, and in the distance I could hear children laughing. Other than that it was pretty quiet. Buchanan is a small town, and there isn't much traffic noise or many wailing sirens to disrupt the peace of a lovely spring afternoon.

The wren stopped singing, and the new silence came just in time. I heard the sound of feet pounding across my lawn and I opened my eyes to see something huge hurtling at me!

Okay, maybe he wasn't huge, but he was a pretty big guy, and he was moving pretty fast. Too fast for me to see much more than a brief impression of him before he barreled into me with a guttural roar and knocked me out of my chair.

I went flying into the grass, and the violent movement jerked George's leash and pulled him off the branch. He started thrashing wildly, really pissed, and I lost my grip on the leash. George whipped the big man right across the face with his long, spiny tail. I'd been hit with that tail before, and I knew from experience it was like getting lashed with a leather bull whip. The guy cried out in pain, but George wasn't done. In a desperate attempt to race to safety the iguana tried to scramble back to the tree using the stranger as a ladder. The guy screamed when George's sharp claws raked his face, and apparently deciding that he was no match for an infuriated two foot long reptile the guy turned and ran back the way he'd come.

George made it to the tree and I pushed myself up from the ground and lunged for the dangling leash, but it was too late. George had made it into the upper branches of my immature tree and was already readying himself for a leap over the fence. On the other side of the fence my neighbor maintains many trees that are much taller than mine, and George was following his instinct to get high and safe.

I took off in pursuit.

My phone started playing "Flirting With Disaster," and I automatically pulled it out of my pocket. Thelma, with her new-found technological skills, downloaded the song to my phone and assigned it as my ringtone for Jack. I was going to make her delete it until she reminded me that Jack would never be standing next to me when he called, so it could be our little secret. Now, I know this was not the time to be answering my phone, but for whatever reason, I seldom ignore Jack's calls.

I answered on the run, my tone a little frantic as I scanned the tree branches for George.

"I don't have time to talk!" I told him breathlessly. "George is gone!"

"Gone?"

I answered him in a heated rush as I reached the neighbor's yard. I knew I was sounding a bit hysterical, but I couldn't help it.

I had lost sight of George, and now I was truly in a panic. "We were out getting some sun and he got startled and took off and I couldn't hold on to the leash and now he's up in the trees and I can't see him and if I don't find him he'll die out on his own and..."

"I'll be right there."

He disconnected. What? He was going to come and help me find George?

I don't understand Jack, never will. It's best, I believe, to not even try. I stuck the phone back in my pocket and peered into the tree.

My neighbor has a large, impressive yard, carefully landscaped, with a row of trees just inside the fence line. His fence only ran up the sides and back of the property, a six foot wooden privacy fence designed to keep riffraff (like me) invisible.

The trees were a mature mixture of oak and maple, the lowest branches well over my head. Even if I spotted George, how was I ever going to climb up to get him?

A ladder maybe. I had a stepladder in the mudroom; would it be tall enough?

First things first. I had to locate him before I came up with a rescue plan.

Spying a green iguana in a sea of green leaves was like trying to find Waldo on a beach covered in red and white striped umbrellas, but fortunately he still had that bright red harness attached, and this early in the season the trees weren't fully leafed out. I focused on finding a patch of red among the leaves and moved slowly around the first tree, peering into the sun dappled branches. My task was made more difficult by the sudden welling of tears in my eyes. I'm sure that was because of the sun. No one cries over a lost iguana, right?

"Are you Rainie?"

The voice was deep and came from just a few feet away; it startled a yelp out of me.

"Who... " I turned to see a very muscular man with longish blonde hair, wearing camouflaged army pants and a tight olive green T shirt that strained over his biceps.

"I'm Pete Randall. Jack sent us." He informed me in a no-nonsense tone. "Us" was another, younger man in jeans and T shirt, more slender than the first but just as well sculpted, and a woman with short-cropped hair wearing black cargo pants and a black T shirt who looked like she just walked out of a mercenary recruiting poster.

"Why?"

"He says you've lost someone, and his ETA is fifteen minutes." Randall spoke like a soldier on a mission. His tone inspired confidence and a desire to be obedient. "We were closer. Can you give us a description of the missing person?"

"Um, yeah, he's about this long," I held

out my hands about two feet apart. "But that isn't counting his tail, which is almost as long. You want to be careful. He can wield it like a bull whip."

Randall's eyes narrowed.

"A tail? Ma'am, just what are we looking for, here? A dog?"

"No! My iguana!"

"Your iguana." The slender guy smirked, but Randall flashed him a look and he hurriedly schooled his expression into something more soldier-like. Clearly he was used to taking orders from his larger companion. Maybe they had served together, and the guy outranked him. Or maybe Randall was just big enough to kick his butt, and had proven it once or twice. Whatever, Randall looked back at me.

"Iguanas can climb, correct?"

"Oh yeah." I looked up at the tree. "He was heading up last time I saw him, but I don't know where he is now."

"Okay, people, fan out!" He ordered, as if there were thirty people with him rather than only two.

They moved out, peering diligently into the trees. Okay, this was a little weird, having a small handful of mercenaries magically appear to help search for my iguana, but far from the weirdest thing I'd ever experienced. I just went with it.

"Hey, one other thing," I called after them. "He's wearing a red leash. Maybe we can see that."

"Got it."

They moved slowly down the tree line, and I stayed with them, desperately searching for a flash of red in all the newly formed leaves. What if he had already made it through the tree tops to the next yard? Or even the next block? What if he came to ground and tried to cross a road and got hit by a car? What if I didn't find him and he got too cold tonight, all alone, far away from his heated cage...

I had to cut off the speculation when I felt a sob threatening to bubble out. I know it may seem crazy, being so attached to a cold-blooded reptile, but I've had George for a long time, and living alone as I do, he is often my only companion. Besides, I'm responsible for his well-being, and it was my fault he was lost. Well, I guess it was really the fault of the guy who had tackled my chair, but if I hadn't had George outside...

"I think I see something!" The woman in black called out. I hustled over to the tree she was standing under and followed her pointing finger up. Sure enough, I could see a strip of red draped over a branch. The problem was, it had to be a good thirty feet up.

"Hey! What the hell are you doing in my yard!" This from my neighbor, Mr. Godsey, who I had actually seen, on occasion, out trimming his lawn with a pair of hand shears to be sure it was perfectly even. I could only imagine how pleased he was to see four people trampling his grass, especially the three wearing combat boots.

"George got loose and..."

"What, your cat or something?" Mr. Godsey cut me off. "I don't care, they should all be shot on sight anyway. Get the hell off my lawn!"

Randall stepped up to Mr. Godsey and planted his feet. "Sir, we have a critical search and rescue mission going on here." I was amazed how he said that with a straight face. "The target has been located and we will retrieve him shortly. The sooner you back out of the area and give us room to work the sooner we will vacate the premises."

"Search and rescue? For a damned cat?" Mr. Godsey had turned so red I feared he might stroke out, but Randall stood his ground. He had planted his feet in that way that soldiers do, with that particular posture that makes them look like a section of immovable wall. He wasn't carrying any guns that I could see, but the set of his jaw and coldness in his eyes declared that he was a dangerous weapon in his own right. He focused that gaze on Mr. Godsey.

"Sir, we will complete our mission.

Please stand down."

Mr. Godsey blinked at Randall. His eyes flicked to me briefly, but settled again on Randall's determined face. Another blink, and he took the time to take in Randall's considerable and intimidating size. He backed off and headed into the house muttering something about calling the cops.

Undaunted by the nearly inaudible threat, Randall went back to giving orders.

"All right, people, let's get on this." He looked up at the red leash in the tree. "Lacey, you'll go up."

Lacey? Really? Could the tough looking woman have a more inappropriate name?

"No problem. Just give me a hike up to that lowest branch."

Randall leaned over, forming a stirrup with hands the size of canned hams so he could lift Lacey into the tree.

"Wait!" I stopped them. "George is scared. When you grab that leash he's going to be lashing with his tail and trying to run."

"Yeah, that's going to make it tough to climb down with him," the slender guy observed. His expression was serious enough, but I could still hear the smirk in his tone.

"Keep an eye on him, I'll go get a pillowcase," I suggested. "If you can get him in it you can tie it off and bring him down in that."

Notice how I didn't offer to climb up and get him myself? It isn't that I wouldn't have, had I been the only choice, but I'm not stupid. Lacey looked far better equipped, and definitely more eager, to scramble up that tree.

"All right, double time!" Randall ordered me as if I was one of his troops. I didn't care, and didn't need to be told to hurry. I took off running for my house.

I got back in record time to find Jack standing under the tree with the others.

"Hey." He greeted me.

"Hey." I handed the pillowcase to Lacey, who wadded it up and stuffed it in one of the generous pockets in her cargo pants.

"Okay, let's do this." She positioned herself under the tree and once again Randall made a stirrup with his hands. She put one foot in, knee bent.

"On three." Randall counted off. "One. Two. Three!" He tossed Lacey up as if she weighed no more than a basketball. At the same time Lacey kicked off, and it seemed like she almost flew into the tree; I suspected they'd done this maneuver before. She landed on the lowest branch with a soft "*oof*" and quickly scrambled around and stood up. She grinned down at us.

"I haven't done any tree climbing in a while. Beats a stone wall any day!"

She started climbing, moving with

surprising stealth in spite of her speed. Geez, did Jack have any *incompetent* friends?

"I can't believe you sent these guys to help me. Do they work for B&E?" I asked Jack, my eyes fixed on Lacey's progress.

"Sometimes," he answered. "I could tell you needed help fast, and I knew these guys were close by, at the Moose today for pool league."

"Thanks. I mean, for sending them to help, and for not making fun of me."

"There's nothing funny about a lost pet." He put an arm around my shoulder and gave me a brief squeeze. In spite of my concern over George, I felt a happy little tingle run through me.

Lacey was moving slower now. She was almost in reach of the leash. She painstakingly moved up another level and straddled a thin branch that bowed precariously under her. Slowly, she stretched out her hand and grasped the red strap. She carefully worked her hand through the loop on the end.

With her other hand she liberated the pillowcase from her pocket. A sudden breeze sprang up, catching the cloth and causing it to flap. Instantly there was a flurry of motion as George, startled by the flapping pillowcase, tried to take flight again.

"Whoa!" Lacey cried out as the leash snapped taut, and I got my first glimpse of

George when his tail lashed out, narrowly missing Lacey's face. Undaunted, she kept a hold on the leash and stuck the pillowcase between her teeth.

There were several heart-stopping moments as they struggled, George trying to go up, Lacey doing her best not to lose her grip on the branch and go down. In spite of the cloth gripped in her teeth, Lacey's cursing was clear to those of us on the ground. She knew words that I had only seen on the internet, and some sounded like they might be in a foreign language, or maybe just made up on the spot.

"Don't grab his tail!" I yelled up at her. "It'll come off!" Iguana's can lose a section of their tail as a defense mechanism, leaving a potential predator holding a twitching piece while the iguana makes it's escape. Of course, it's terribly stressful on the animal, and it was best avoided.

There was a renewed burst of cursing from above, and I thought I heard something like "shove that damn tail down it's throat..." but then Lacey had a grip behind George's head and she was shoving him into the pillowcase, whipping her head back and forth to avoid the violently lashing tail, and finally she had him all in there and was twisting the top of the bag closed.

She scrambled down one handed, making it look like the most natural thing in the world. She straddled the lowest branch and dangled the thrashing bag down. Jack stepped forward and accepted it from her.

"Thanks, Lacey."

"No problem, Jack." She grinned and pushed herself off the tree branch, executing a perfect two-point landing that would have made an Olympic athlete proud. There were a couple of red welts on her face from George's tail, but she didn't seem to notice.

"Can we get back to our pool game now?" Randall looked at his watch. "Another seven minutes and we'll have to forfeit."

"Go."

"Double time," Randall ordered his troops, and they took off running. No handshakes, no big "thank yous" or even much acknowledgement of how much they'd inconvenienced themselves to help a friend of Jack's they'd never met before. I wondered if they had driven over or just ran all the way; the Moose wasn't much more than a mile away, and I was pretty sure that crew could do a seven minute mile without even breaking a sweat. It sort of made me wish I was in better shape, but then, that would probably require long hours of hard work, and for what? I really didn't need to run that fast or that far very often...

Jack held up the pillowcase, possibly to pull my attention back to the here and now. He seemed to be getting used to my frequent mental wanderings. George had gone still, and I hoped he was just playing it safe, waiting for the next round of danger.

"We'd better get him inside before he gets any further traumatized."

I nodded and reached for the bag, but Jack shook his head. "I'll carry him."

He headed for my house, and with a shrug I followed him.

## Chapter Two

I got George settled in his cage, and after an inspection to be sure he had no obvious wounds, I turned the lights off in his cage and covered the front with a blanket so he could rest. Stress is a common killer of captive animals, and needs to be reduced as quickly as possible after a trauma.

Jack followed me into the kitchen.

"So how did he get away?" He asked. "You're usually pretty careful."

"I know, but I wasn't expecting to get tackled this morning." Funny, I had forgotten all about that guy. It's weird how your brain can focus on one thing to the exclusion of all else, even things that would be best remembered.

"Tackled? By who? Where?"

"I don't know who, but out in the back yard. George and I were just sitting there, getting some sun, and this guy came running out of nowhere and knocked me out of my chair. It was pretty weird."

"Weird?" Jack looked pissed. "When

were you planning to tell me about this?"

"I don't think I was really planning to, it just popped out." I grinned. "Lucky I had George with me; he's my hero! He whipped that guy in the face and just about scratched his eyes out!" I laughed. "The guy took off running pretty quick after that."

"Rainie, this isn't funny!"

"Oh, come on. Don't go getting all bad-ass protective, Jack. It was just a strange random incident, I wasn't hurt, and George is back in his cage safe and sound. Don't be making a big deal out of it."

"Rainie, have you forgotten there's a guy out there trying to kill me?"

"What does that have to do with this?"

"I told you before, if he can't get to me, he might well try to get at me through you."

"And I asked you then, why would he do that? It doesn't make any sense."

"Look, Rainie, it's standard operating procedure. If you can't get at your target directly, go through the people he cares about the most."

"Yeah?" I felt my face flushing. "Are you saying you care about me?"

"Are you saying you don't already know that?"

"Well, I... um, I guess I never really thought about it."

"I admit I'm not good at talking about

my feelings and all that, but come on, Rainie. Do you think I come running for just anyone's lost pet?"

"Gee, I feel so special." And uncomfortable. Jack isn't the only one who doesn't like to spend a lot of time talking about feelings.

"I need you to take this seriously," Jack insisted. "Did you get any kind of look at the guy?"

"No." I thought about it, but all I could remember was an impression of big, and fast.

"Do you remember those pictures I showed you? Could it have been him?"

"I don't think so."

Someone has been trying to kill Jack, beginning with burning down his house, with him in it. Jack had shown me a picture of the guy. At the time I had been pretty sure I had seen him before, but I hadn't been able to remember where. "I think I would have recognized him."

"Great. That means there are for sure more than one of them."

Belatedly, I felt a thrill of fear. "Do you really think that guy was one of them? Do you think he was going to kill me?"

"Maybe. I don't know." Jack put his hands on my shoulders and met my eyes, his expression as deadly serious as I've ever seen it. "You need to be watching all the time,

Rainie. Maybe I should move in here for a while..."

"No!" I was shaking my head and moving away from him. "Not a chance. I'm not going to disrupt my whole life over this."

"Getting killed would be a hell of a disruption."

"We don't even know for sure if that's what's going on. No, I'll be fine. I'll just pay more attention."

"You should buy a gun..."

"Uh uh, no way. I don't carry a gun. That's *your* bad-ass job."

"You can be bad-assed when you need to be."

"Me? Nope, I'm just a peace-loving caregiver who likes to write poems and maybe track down a dead-beat dad now and then."

"Even if it means running them over with your car or shooting them in the knee. Yep, you're right, nothing bad-assed about you."

"Jack, I can reach my hand into my purse and come out with a tissue, a client's med list, or a pen and a notebook without even having to look, but my life skills don't include remembering to grab a weapon in a life or death situation."

"Don't be ridiculous. You've done it before."

"That doesn't mean I want to make a

habit of it! I don't want to live the kind of life that requires deadly force to get through a day."

An odd look passed across Jack's face, as rapidly as the lights flickering off and on during a thunderstorm. Then it was gone, and he offered me a crooked smile.

"Sometimes the universe doesn't offer you a choice."

"The universe?" I laughed. "Are you getting all spiritual on me now?"

"I just thought I'd try speaking to you in your mother's language, maybe get you to understand."

"Except you are not my mom, and besides, she would never advocate me carrying a gun."

Jack stared at me for a minute, and I swear I could see him mentally counting to ten. I could almost see the numbers rolling up behind his eyes, like an old-fashioned gas pump ticker.

"All right," he said at last. "A Taser then. No deadly force, just enough stopping power to give you time to run."

"A Taser? Is it legal to carry one of those?"

"It is with a carry-concealed permit."

"I'm not going to do that. They fingerprint you for that."

"So?"

"So, I may not be as paranoid as my mom, but I don't want my fingerprints on file in some national database."

"Why not? Are you planning the perfect murder sometime in the future?"

"No! It just seems... invasive somehow."

"You do know they'll have to fingerprint you when you apply for you private investigator's license."

"I haven't decided yet if I want to do that, either."

"You're just going to remain an assistant?"

"I hardly see what difference it makes. I seem to get in plenty of trouble without a license!"

Jack sighed. "We're getting way off topic here. The point is that there may be a couple of guys out to do you harm, and if you won't let me protect you, then you need the means to protect yourself."

"I'm not helpless."

"Oh, I know." Jack grinned. "I never have been interested in the helpless female type."

I felt my breath come a little short at that. What did he mean? That he was interested in me... in what way? I stared at him for a long, uncomfortable moment, wanting to break the silence with something witty or sarcastic, but nothing came to mind.

Abruptly, Jack laughed, and I realized he was just teasing me again. Damn his mean streak!

"All right, Rainie, then how about you keep your pepper spray handy. You still have the one I gave you for your keychain, right?"

"Sure... somewhere... "

"Somewhere? It's supposed to be on your keychain."

"I know, but it's too bulky, when I stick my keys in my pocket it bulges it out and looks silly."

Again, that long "I'm-counting-to-ten-so-I-don't-say-something-I'll-regret" stare. I interrupted him around number seven.

"Okay, okay, I'll put the pepper spray on my key chain."

"Thank you." Jack kissed me on the forehead, and I got a little shiver that was a totally inappropriate response to the brotherly gesture. "Are you going into the office today?"

I think I might have made a funny little face. The office in question was the Niles, Michigan branch of B&E Security, a firm that offered everything from PI work to bodyguards to consultations on complete security set ups for home and business. Jack and I both worked for them, though my job description was a lot less dangerous than his. At least, on paper.

Anyway, I usually do go to the office on

Mondays, or do field work for B&E, but honestly I had been thinking about just blowing it off today. I don't know why that made me feel guilty; it isn't as if Jack is my boss. I guess it's just that it sounded so... lazy.

"I'm not sure..."

"You have interviews today?"

"No... actually, it's just too nice out to work. I thought I'd take the day off. Why?"

"No big deal. I just have some paperwork to drop off there, but I have to be in Benton Harbor for an appointment and I'm running a little late."

Right. Running late because of the Great Iguana Rescue, the fault of yours, truly. I don't need to be slapped upside the head with a guilt trip to recognize one. I hid a sigh with a fake smile. "I can run it over for you, no problem."

"Be honest, it is a problem... but I really appreciate it." He went out to his truck to get the paperwork. Anyone else, having recognized and even acknowledged they were putting me out, would probably need a bit of coaxing, even if I did owe them a favor. That's one thing I like about Jack; he doesn't waste time on those silly social games.

"Promise me you'll stay alert, and if *anything* suspicious happens - no matter how insignificant it seems - call me, okay?"

"Okay." I lied, rather easily I'm afraid. I refuse to get in the habit of calling Jack about every creepy thing that happens in my life; lately, if I did that, I'd just have to wear a Bluetooth headset and keep him in the loop around the clock. Not going to happen.

I accepted the file and grabbed my keys.

"Hi, Belinda." I greeted B&E's office manager and go-to person. Belinda amazed me; she was one of those self-confident people that never seemed to be embarrassed or shy or intimidated by anything or anyone. She was tall, big-boned and gorgeous, as well as smart, capable and as open as a library book. You might assume from this description that I really like her, and you would be right.

"Hi, Rainie. Are you looking for a new assignment?"

"Actually I was just bringing you some paperwork Jack needed dropped off. It's just so nice out today, I was planning to play hooky."

"So you drove all the way over here just to do a favor for Jack?"

"Yeah, but only because I owed him one."

"Really?" Belinda waggled her perfectly sculpted eyebrows suggestively. "What did he do for you?"

I laughed. "Nothing as fun as you seem to imagine. He helped me get George out of a tree."

"Your iguana? What was he doing in a

tree?"

"I had him out for some sun and he got startled and took off."

"What startled him? A rampant squirrel?" Belinda grinned.

"I think it was when I fell out of my chair. Or maybe it was when the big scary guy pushed me, I'm not sure."

"What?" Belinda looked as if she wasn't sure now if she should be amused or not. "Are you serious?"

"Yeah, but it's no big deal. I'm fine, and George is safely back in his cage."

"But why did some guy push you out of your chair?"

"I have no idea. Some random crazy, I hope."

"Rainie, you live in Buchanan, not New York City. There aren't all that many random crazy guys running around. What are the odds one of them would pick on you?"

I sighed. "I know, that's what Jack said. Look, I already got a lecture from him, and I promised to watch my back, just in case it wasn't random. Let's not beat it into the ground, okay?"

"Fine with me; you're a big girl, you can decide for yourself how freaked out to be."

"Thanks... I think. Anyway, if you don't have anything pressing, I'm going to take off."

"Since you're already here, do you think

you could just put in a half hour or so? I just got an email from Rachel; she's on a hot lead and she needs some numbers looked up."

I almost moaned aloud; there were few things more dull than running phone numbers through the reverse phone look ups. On the other hand, I really liked working for B&E, and they were incredibly flexible about my hours.

I couldn't hide a small sigh as I reluctantly nodded.

"Sure, I can do that."

"It's not a big list," Belinda assured me. "I'll send it to your email. You'll be out of here in plenty of time for some fun in the sun, I promise."

I went back to the computer room where the other PI assistants and I spend most of our time. I went to the computer in the corner, my favorite spot, and tapped it to bring up the screen. I signed into my company email and opened the list of numbers. Belinda was right; it was a relatively short list, only sixteen numbers. I could breeze through them in no time.

I got started without a last longing look at the sunshine beaming outside the window. Well, maybe just one quick yearning glance...

I finished up in just under a half hour and scooted out the door with a quick wave at Belinda. I didn't stop to chat again, not wanting to take a chance that she might find some other rush task she needed me to perform.

When I got home I first lifted the corner of the sheet to check on George. He blinked at me, then crept up to the top branch of his cage as he usually did, waiting expectantly for me to open the hatch so he could climb up on his shelf. He didn't look shocky or traumatized in the least, and I suspected I had been more upset by his adventure than he had been.

"I think I'm going to go for a bike ride," I informed him. He didn't say anything, just sat there, as inscrutable as Confucius. "I think you should stay in your cage and rest a bit more, just in case." He didn't object, so I let the sheet fall back into place and went to get my bike out.

I rode through the quiet streets, waving to the occasional neighbor out working in the yard, enjoying the breeze in my face. Riding in Buchanan is not as easy as you might think; the town is built in a shallow valley, actually somewhat like a bowl, so no matter which direction you go there is eventually a hill to climb. Or coast down, which was my favorite.

I was doing just that, free-wheeling down Front Street, heading into downtown, worried that I might be rolling over the posted twenty-five mile an hour speed limit but loving the illusion that I was moving along at a hundred miles an hour, when I spotted a guy sitting in a car in the lot next to McCoy Creek park. I wouldn't have noticed him if not for the sun glinting off the lens of a pair of binoculars that he seemed to have pointed in my direction.

I looked hard at him as I sailed by, and he dropped the glasses below the level of the windshield and deliberately looked away. I braked hard and turned into the lot. I wanted to know who the hell he was, and why he was watching me!

I almost missed the turn and skidded hard, barely catching myself from going over. I got the bike stopped, but by then the guy had already started his car and was headed for the other exit to the lot. His car was an old, well-used Buick, dark blue, with a few scrapes and rust spots but nothing too distinctive. Belatedly I thought to look for a plate number; I saw enough to know they were Indiana plates, but I was too far away to make out much more.

Damn it. I stared after him, hands on hips. Who was that guy? Why was he watching me?

Suddenly I laughed. What made me so sure he was watching me?

I was being ridiculous, acting paranoid because of Jack's dire warning.

Then again, could that have been one of

the guys after Jack? Was I being stalked?

I finally shook my head. I could stand and speculate all day, but that wouldn't get me any closer to an answer. It was just too pretty a day to worry about it. I got back on my bike and headed for Next To You, the store owned by Thelma and my sister, Brenda.

Thelma would be working today. That's how she spent her days when I wasn't with her, ostensibly as her caregiver.

I walked my bike the last block to the shop and parked it next to a lamp post, unwrapping the chain lock from the frame. My bike was relatively new, but of the retro variety: single speed, upright handlebars, and a wide seat that didn't make me feel as if I was being impaled on a dull blade when I sat on it.

I wrapped the chain around the frame and through the back wheel. It isn't as if downtown Buchanan is a high crime area, but why tempt someone to steal it? It wasn't much, but it was mine.

The bell over the door tinkled merrily when I went in, and Thelma turned at the sound, smiling a welcome. She usually preferred to wear jeans and T shirts, often with a rock & roll theme, but for work she was wearing a neatly fitted pair of black slacks and a white, button up blouse with lace at the collar.

"Hi, Rainie! What's up with you today?"

"I was out for a bike ride, thought I'd stop and see how the store was doing."

"Pretty good." She indicated a pile of boxes. "I'm just putting out the summer stuff, packing away the cold weather items."

"Gee, sounds like so much fun."

"Beats hanging around the senior center watching my friends grow old."

I laughed with her, in total agreement, and decided to hang out for a while, helping her sort and hang clothes.

Next to You sold quality used clothing, the initial inventory coming from my obsessive-compulsive sister's room sized closet. She had had an epiphany one day, and decided she shouldn't own so much stuff when others were doing without. The result was Next To You, which donated a percentage of profits to charity and also provided clothes to the homeless or down-at-the-heel job seekers.

They kept the store stocked by purchasing used items from customers, usually just for store credit. The place was doing surprisingly well... or maybe not so surprising, considering Thelma was in charge.

At quarter to five Thelma tossed a last empty box into the back room and dusted her hands off. She peered out the front window. "He's early."

Morty, Thelma's very old and no-longer-very-competent-behind-the-wheel chauffer, was waiting at the curb.

"Want to go out to dinner?" Thelma asked. "Your bike will fit in Morty's trunk, and he can take us over to Sonny's."

"Hm, I don't know..." I glanced out at Morty, who was sitting behind the wheel of the idling Lincoln Continental, staring off into the distance with rheumy eyes. He had one hand draped across the steering wheel, and it was trembling like a leaf in a high wind. He couldn't hear very well anymore, and his eyesight was failing in spite of cataract surgery and coke bottle lens glasses with four-inch frames that covered half of his wrinkled old face. Morty was ninety-something, and probably should have given up driving at least a year ago, but on the other hand Sunny's was just up Front Street, maybe a mile away, the speed limit restricted to twenty-five miles per hour. How dangerous could it be?

"Sure, why not?" I grinned at Thelma and we went out to load up my bike.

Morty got us there in one piece, although once or twice I thought we might share paint samples with a parked car. He joined us for dinner, and had Thelma and I both laughing throughout the meal. Thelma claimed she kept Morty on because he was so dependent on the cash she paid him, but really I think it's because of his sense of humor.

Thelma loves to laugh, and Morty can tell a one-liner almost as good as Rodney Dangerfield; he has ninety years of funny stories filed away in his still nimble brain, and he seemed to have one for every occasion.

We chatted over our meals, a Greek salad for me (anchovies, yum!) and fried chicken for Thelma and Morty. Sonny's used to be well known for its fried chicken, but when the original owners retired and sold the restaurant, they hadn't included their recipe in the deal. Both Thelma and Morty lamented over the lackluster flavor of their meal.

"But you *know* it isn't like it used to be," I pointed out. "So why didn't you order something else?"

"Because I like to remember how it used to be," Morty grinned. "I can't taste much anymore anyway, so I eat this and imagine it tastes good."

I smiled. "How's that working for you?"

"Not too bad," Morty winked at me. "At my age, imagination is about the only way you still get the good stuff."

Thelma and I both laughed at his innuendo.

"Speaking of good stuff, how's that boyfriend of yours, Thelma?"

"I wouldn't go so far as to call him my boyfriend yet. We've only gone out a couple of times."

"Twice, huh?" Morty cocked his head at her. "So I saw on TV that there's something nowadays called the 'three date rule,' says you gotta go out three times before you go to the bedroom so you aren't considered a loose woman. You going along with that or are you holding out for marriage?"

"Morty!" I admonished him. "What a question to ask a lady!"

"Hey, that's no lady, that's Thelma!" He chortled.

"I'd kick your ass if you still had one!" Thelma shot back at him. "Wouldn't be able to find it anyway; one of these days I'm thinking you'll just hook your belt loops over your ears to hold them pants up."

"At least I dress my age. Who you trying to kid with those rock & roll clothes, anyway?"

"You dress your age, all right," Thelma shot back. "When's the last time you updated your wardrobe, sometime before cars were invented?"

They exchanged insults for a few minutes, sounding like a couple of elderly fourth graders, stopping only when the waitress came to clear our plates.

"Is everything okay here?" She asked, a little "tone" in her voice. Maybe she feared the geriatrics were going to break out into a knock-down brawl in the middle of the restaurant, smashing tables and glassware like a couple of cowboys in a western movie.

"Sure honey," Thelma grinned innocently. "How about coffee all around?"

"Regular or decaf?"

"Regular!" Morty ordered. "I need the caffeine to keep my heart beat from slowing down too much."

The waitress smiled uncertainly and hurried off, maybe thinking Morty was serious and worried she might have to perform CPR if she didn't get him the coffee quick enough.

"Did you hear about that bank robbery over in Niles?" Morty asked after the coffee was served.

"No, when was that?"

"Last week. Took some people hostage and everything."

"No kidding?" I was appalled. "I haven't watched the news lately."

"Thing is, that robber dropped some of the money, and when he bent over to pick it up his mask fell off. He asked one of the hostages if he saw his face, and when the guy admitted he had, the robber shot him!"

"Wow!" Thelma blinked. "How did I not hear about this?"

"I don't know," Morty shrugged. "Anyway, the robber turned to a woman and asked her if *SHE* saw his face. The woman shook her head and said, 'No, but my husband did.'"

It took a second, but then the punch line hit me like it was meant to, and I started laughing so hard my eyes and nose started running. Thelma looked like she might be about to wet her pants. Morty just sat smiling, clearly pleased with himself. The joke itself wasn't all that funny; Morty's delivery, and his convincing us it was a true story, was.

"Morty," I asked when I finally had control of myself, "Where do you get this stuff?"

"Humor is all around you if you pay attention," he winked at me. "And it helps if you read the "Reader's Digest" when you're sitting in a waiting room."

"You missed your calling. You should have been a stand-up comedian."

"Maybe so," he nodded. "But I don't think I could do that now. Hell, nowadays I even have to sit down to pee!"

That got us laughing again, and the waitress was eyeing us suspiciously, maybe thinking we'd snuck a flask of whiskey in to add to our coffee.

We finished our coffee and Thelma paid the check, leaving the waitress a bigger tip than she'd earned. We piled back into the car and Morty drove me home. I unloaded my bike.

"Hey, it's getting dark already. Be

careful, Morty."

"We'll be okay. I've got good insurance." With that not so comforting reassurance he winked and backed out of the driveway.

## Chapter Three

The next morning greeted me with a chill rain, and I was glad I had gotten a bike ride in the day before. I opted for jeans and a T shirt but refused to go back to my tennis shoes; I slipped into my thin sandals and called it good. It was, after all, spring.

I was pleased to see that George was still in apparently good health, and, when I arrived as usual at Thelma's at eight o'clock, so was she.

She greeted me with a cup of fresh coffee, and I couldn't help noticing she was a little more dressed up than usual for one of our days together. She was wearing a royal blue blouse tucked into relatively new jeans, and she was even wearing dangly earrings.

"You look like you're dressed for work today," I commented. "Are we going someplace special?"

"No... well, actually, I want to take you to lunch."

"Okay... " I waited, knowing there must be something more. Her normal T shirt and scruffy jeans were fine for the places we usually went for lunch.

"I asked Gary to join us. You said you want to meet him, right?"

"Of course! That's great!"

She had met Gary a few weeks ago, and they had gone out a couple of times. Thelma was playing it cool, but I could tell she was smitten with him. I was anxious to meet the man who could make Thelma blush like a schoolgirl.

"I told him we'd meet at the Nugget in Niles at twelve-thirty, if that's okay with you."

"You're the boss," I reminded her with a smile.

"Right." She rolled her eyes. "So what do you want to do in the meantime?"

"I don't know. It's too wet out for a walk. Do you have any shopping to do?"

"Not for me, but that reminds me, I haven't taken anything over to the food bank for a while. How about we do some grocery shopping for RAM?"

"Great idea!" RAM was Redbud Area Ministries, a local charity run with the cooperation of several area churches. Thelma shoved a roll of cash in her pocket and grabbed a jacket and we were out the door.

Gary wasn't at all what I expected. The best word I can think of to describe him is "robust." He was tall and broad, a bit of his muscle turning to fat, with a thick head of silver hair brushed back from a high forehead. His nose was classic Roman, his mouth full and eager to smile. All in all, he was a very handsome guy.

Even better, he had a great sense of humor and a sharp wit that he wasn't afraid to wield. He started right off when he shook my hand.

"You know, I was nervous as a long-tailed cat in a roomful of rocking chairs about this lunch."

"Oh? Why is that?"

"Well, this is sort of like a job interview, right? I need your approval if I want to keep seeing this fine lady."

I laughed. "Thelma doesn't need my or anyone else's approval to do what she chooses to do."

"Okay, maybe she doesn't need it, but she wants it, isn't that right?" He winked at Thelma, who blushed.

"Well, it would be nice if you two could get along."

"There, you see? I know an order when I hear one. The thing is, I haven't had to sit a job interview for a long time. I tried to remember how I impressed the bosses at my successful interviews, but the memory is just too dim. Guess I have to wing it."

I smiled at him. "Maybe it would be better if we just talk a bit, and get to know each other."

"Oh, sure, like one of those "new age" type things, get in touch with our feelings and all that stuff?"

It took me a minute, but I finally realized he was putting me on, at least a little. I had no doubt that Thelma did want my approval, and Gary knew it. But he was trying to make light of it, and I liked that.

"Yes, and later we'll do some trust exercises," I said, going along with the theme.

"Right, or maybe sit in a circle and sing camp songs, really get the bonding going."

"Gary, you're too much," Thelma giggled.

"I know," he nodded. "Now, all kidding aside," he leaned across the table and looked me in the eye, but I could still see that spark of humor there, and I suspected he wasn't really about to be all that serious. "I really like this woman, and I'm willing to go the extra mile for her. So, if you do find something about me you really don't like, you speak up, and I'll see what I can do about changing it. Don't get me wrong, there are some things that are so fundamental about me I couldn't change them any more than I could change the color of my eyes, but I'm not so set in stone about other things. I learned not to fart in church and how to use a tissue rather than pick my nose, so I'm trainable, okay?"

I laughed, I couldn't help it. His delivery of these lines reminded me of Morty, all matter of fact and serious. "Well, that's good to know. Are you housebroken?"

"Mostly. I do break a dish now and then, and living alone like I do I sort of got in the habit of burping pretty much whenever I want in my own living room, but I can change. I've reached that age where it's better for my prostate if I sit down to pee, so I don't have any really bad habits, like leaving the toilet seat up."

"Oh, that is so much more information than I really needed!" But I couldn't help it, he still had me laughing.

"Maybe I should have warned you that Gary doesn't take himself too seriously," Thelma grinned.

"I wouldn't expect you to spend time with someone who did." I looked back at Gary. "Thelma tells me you recently retired," I said. "What did you do for a living?"

"Ah, the inquest begins."

"Interview, not inquest."

"Okay, fair enough. I owned a construction business, pretty successful, but my only kid decided to be an architect and didn't want to keep it going. Worked out for the best; I sold out before the housing market crashed and managed to put away a pretty nice nest egg."

"You were lucky. A lot of people lost everything."

"Don't I know it. I had a few good friends that went down with the ship. Hell of a thing, trying to rebuild your life after sixty."

"You were married once, right?"

"I was," Gary nodded. "Almost thirty years. Then one day my wife announced she wanted to move to Colorado to be near my son and the grandkids. This was when my business was still going full throttle. I told her there was no way, I couldn't just close up and start all over, I was already fifty-three years old. She said fine, she'd just go without me.

"So, that's what she did. She was a secretary... oh, sorry, I guess they like to be called 'office assistants' or whatever now... anyway, she moved out there and found herself a new job and never looked back."

"Wow, that's pretty harsh."

"I thought so at the time. Hell, I was devastated, mourned that lady for almost a year, trying to convince her to come back. Then one evening I was watching TV, and I wanted to take my socks off, but I didn't feel like walking all the way into the bedroom to put them in the hamper. Gladys was real strict about stuff like that, she'd really let me have it if she found a sock on the floor. But then it occurred to me: Gladys wasn't there. I could throw my socks wherever the hell I wanted! So I took them off and put them on the floor until I was ready to go to bed, and *then* I took them to the hamper. It was maybe the most liberating moment of my adult life!" He laughed heartily. "I guess I never really realized how miserable that woman was making me until she was long gone!"

"Oh, that's sad!" Thelma said, but belied her words by laughing.

"Naw, what's sad is it took me a year to figure it out!"

There was no doubt, I liked this guy. In fact, I liked him so much I couldn't help a little twinge of jealousy; I know it's selfish, but I like being Thelma's best friend, and I didn't much like the idea of being replaced by this man.

I glanced at Thelma and saw the adoration in her eyes when she gazed at Gary, and for just a moment I decided I didn't like him so much at all.

*Oh, knock it off!* That little voice inside me commanded. *Thelma has room in her heart for both of you.*

Of course she did. I pushed the jealousy down and concentrated on enjoying lunch.

On Wednesday I headed straight to B&E at eight o'clock, feeling virtuous about making up for blowing it off on Monday. I planned to spend the whole day on B&E stuff to make up for the lost time.

I breezed down the hall to Belinda's office to say good morning and see what was new. I stopped short when I saw that her door was closed; in all the time I have been working here I've never known her to close it. I hesitated, but I didn't hear any raised voices or bodies being slammed against the wall, so I thought it was safe enough to knock. I tapped lightly.

"Come in," she called out.

I opened the door to see her sitting behind her desk with one hand outstretched like a traffic cop. "Stop! Don't come any closer..." she abruptly spun her chair away and sneezed hard into a tissue, once twice, then a third time. She blew her nose and finally turned back with a sigh. Her eyes were red and she looked a little pale under her always perfect makeup.

"We have the plague," she smiled thinly. "At least, if feels like it. We have two detectives and three assistants out with this nasty flu, and now I have it, too. I just came in to get things organized and then I'm heading home."

"Oh yuk! Maybe I should get out of here..."

"No, you're safe enough. Harry had the cleaning crew come in last night and sterilize everything, and no one else has been here. In fact, I really need you today; things are getting backed up!"

"Okay, I planned to put in a full day."

"Good." Belinda pointed at a pile of folders on the corner of her desk. "There's a whole lot that needs to be done, stacked in order of priority. I'm sure you won't get through it all, but do what you can."

"Sure." I picked up the folders and backed away, not wanting to breathe in Typhoid Belinda's germs. "Is it all computer work?" I tried to keep the distaste out of my voice, but Belinda heard it anyway.

"Yeah, I'm afraid most of it is. There is one interesting one though, the bottom of the pile."

I pulled out the bottom folder and flipped it open to find a couple of sheets of paper that were clipped together. The top sheet was a standard intake form with the new clients name, address and other vital information.

"The client is Carrie Germaine. She hired us to look for her long lost father."

"Really?" I scanned the sheet quickly. This was a little more interesting than data base runs.

"Here's the thing: she doesn't know much of anything about him. Her mother remarried when she was little, and her stepfather adopted her. Her mother was very bitter about her ex-husband, said he was an abusive and scary guy, and refused to share any information with Carrie."

"If he's that bad, why would she want to find him?"

"Because she wants to know if it's all true or if her mother was lying to her all those years. She admitted to me that her mother had a tendency to stretch the truth. Her mother passed away last year, and now Carrie has a daughter of her own. She wants to know the truth about her biological father."

"Sure, I can see that. I mean, what if the guy was a talented musician or a serial killer? You'd definitely want to know if you should be buying your kid a guitar or hiding the kitchen knives, right?"

Belinda laughed, but it was short lived, cut off by an ominous sounding cough that made me back up a step into the hallway. She recovered, blew her nose, and finally answered me."I guess so. Anyway, like I said, she doesn't know much about him, not even his first name. The only real clue she has is that once he came to Kentucky to see her, but her mother refused to let him in the house. Carrie remembers him shouting "I came all the way from Buchanan to see her!" Buchanan rings true for Carrie; she remembers living there in kindergarten, because they were working on getting her to memorize her address and phone number."

"And that's all she has to go on?"

"It gets worse." Belinda sneezed and blew again, and I couldn't help noticing she was sounding raspier by the minute. "She doesn't even know for sure if it was Buchanan, Michigan. She's already searched Buchanan, Ohio, and next she'll try Illinois if we don't find him."

"Huh. I never realized there were so many cities named Buchanan."

"Me neither. Apparently he was a popular president, or at least generous with the civic donations. The only other thing she has to go on is an old photo... that's the next page."

I flipped to the picture. It was black and white, and not very clear, a faxed photocopy of a photograph. The young man was carefully posed, smiling widely for the camera.

"This looks like a senior picture; you know, like from a yearbook."

"That's what I thought. It's the only picture Carrie has of him. She thinks it was taken in the late seventies or early eighties. In any case, Carrie doesn't have a lot of money, so we can't put a whole lot into this. The only way I can think to start is to look up divorce decrees for the time that involved a child, and make a list of names. Maybe one will pop for her."

"Why not take this picture around town? A lot of people in Buchanan have lived there their whole lives. If this guy lived there, even thirty years ago, someone might recognize him."

"Wow, that's a great idea, Rainie! Why didn't I think of that?"

"Because you didn't grow up in a small town; it wouldn't occur to you that everyone knows everyone else."

"That's such a great idea," Belinda spun away and sneezed again. "You would be the perfect person to take the photo around, since you know who would have been here thirty years ago."

"I'd love to. Anything to get me away from the computer."

"Yeah, but remember, that one is a low priority; we just got it in yesterday. Work on some of the other stuff first, please?"

"Sure," I sighed, watching my door to freedom swinging closed in my face.

"Okay, great. I'm out of here." Belinda grabbed her purse and I backed away before she could come near me. "Harry is in his office, and there's a couple of other people around, but you should have the computer room to yourself."

"Okay with me. Hope you feel better soon," I said as I backed down the hall.

"I will. I'll be back as soon as the fever breaks and I'm not contagious anymore. In the meantime I'll have my cell and my computer, and I can still help from home if you need me."

We went our separate ways, her to her sick bed, and me to the computer room.

I sat down at my familiar computer in the corner, comforted by the strong antiseptic smell in the room. My mother would disapprove of the chemicals, but I was glad of anything that would keep from me being reduced to a sneezing, coughing, feverish wreck. I truly hate being sick.

I opened the folder and started plugging away at the stack of items needing to be done. I realized several of them were simple data base searches, so, clever me, I used three of the other computers to run them while I worked on reverse phone look ups. Periodically I would make the rounds of the computers and check progress or narrow the search results. As I finished each assignment I filled out the report forms and filed them, pleased to see the undone pile getting shorter as the day went on.

The building was creepy quiet with so few people in it, but without interruptions I was getting through the stack at a good clip. At two o'clock my tummy growled, and I realized I hadn't taken a lunch break. Well, I'd put in a very productive six hours, so I wasn't about to feel guilty for knocking off for the day.

I was about to put the incomplete folder away when I remembered Carrie and her long lost father. I didn't really think there was much hope of finding the guy with so little to go on, but the idea intrigued me. I pulled the report and photograph and took it with me. I could grab a quick lunch somewhere and then stop a couple of places to ask about it.

I drove to McDonalds and got a big salad, ignoring my mother's voice in my head warning me of all the toxic chemical preservatives the fast food chain used to keep the salads looking pretty for days on end. It wasn't that I didn't share my mother's aversion to chemicals; it was more that lately I simply didn't have time to avoid them. Our environment is saturated with them, and it takes a lot of effort to avoid them completely. I figure if I'm only exposing myself to them a couple of times a week and going organic the rest of the time my body should manage to process it out... I hoped.

I pulled into a parking spot and ate while I considered who I should speak to first about the mystery photograph.

There are a lot of people in Buchanan who have lived here for thirty years or more; the key was to think of someone who would have had contact with a lot of people. I considered and rejected several possibilities. The retired police chief would have been good, but he was probably not back from his winter in Arizona. Very few shop owners were still around from thirty years ago; most of the old stores had closed and been replaced by out-of-towners.

Then I had it: my friend Gina's mother had always been very active in the community, serving on the city council and several committees devoted to the betterment of Buchanan. There were probably not many people in town she hadn't had a reason to talk to over the years.

I pulled up Gina's number on my cell.

"Hello?" She answered after several rings, sounding as raspy as Belinda had. What the hell, was there an epidemic going around? Maybe I needed to get a surgical mask, or better yet, a full biohazard suit...

"Hi, Gina, it's Rainie. Are you okay?"

"Oh sure. Just busy dying..." she broke off in a coughing fit that left her wheezing. I heard a kid crying in the background, and I suspected one or both of her young sons were sick, as well.

"I'm sorry, this is a bad time..."

"No, it's okay. Not like I was resting or anything. Both boys and Rick are home sick."

"Oh boy." I had heard horror stories about how difficult sick husbands could be; I had been pretty fortunate during my short marriage to Tommy. I don't remember him ever being sick.

"Oh boy is right. I'm thinking I'd like to check into a hotel for a night or two and leave them on their own... anyway, what's up?"

"Actually, I'm working another case..."

"Of course you are. You never call just to chat anymore."

"I'm sorry, Gina, I know I've been terrible about that..."

"Yeah, yeah, don't worry about it. I'm just bitchy 'cause I feel like crap. People get busy; I haven't really called you much either, right? So what can I help with?"

"I was hoping to talk to your mother, actually. I have an old picture I want her to look at, to see if she can ID the guy in it."

"Yeah?" I lost her for a minute when she went into another coughing spasm. "Sounds intriguing, is it something you can tell me about?"

"Sure, but maybe we should get together for coffee... when you're feeling better..."

"That's a plan, and I'll hold us both to it. You ready for Mom's number?"

"Yep."

She recited it and I wrote it down. "Thanks, Gina. I hope you feel better soon."

"Me too. I'll call you when I'm functioning again and you can tell me what this is all about."

"I'll look forward to it." And I meant it. It was true, we had drifted apart since high school, but Gina could still make me laugh.

I disconnected and called her mother,

who sounded thrilled to hear from me.

"You come right on over, Rainie! You remember where the house is?"

"Of course! I spent enough Saturdays there growing up."

"Yes, you did. You girls about drove me to distraction, but I think I'd prefer all that giggling and nonsense to the quiet I have now. Anyway, come on over, I'll make coffee."

I disconnected, and with a cup of coffee as incentive made record time to Gina's mother's house on the end of Cayuga Street.

It was a small house with a large enclosed front porch that I remember sleeping on in the summer when the nights got hot; there hadn't been any air conditioning. The many ground floor windows had also been convenient when we were older; we had snuck out many nights after Gina's folks were asleep for the night. It had all seemed like an adventure at the time, but when I thought back now on the things we had done, I wanted to smack my young self upside the head. What had we been thinking? The answer came to me immediately: we hadn't been thinking, of course. We were stupid teenagers who thought we already knew everything the adults had to teach us, and we were out to prove to the world how grown up we were. It's a wonder, looking back, that we survived. I don't know if we had angels, Karma, the Fates or just plain luck on our side, but if I ever figure that out I'll be sure to give them a big thank you. And if I ever have kids of my own, I'll put alarms on their windows.

"Rainie, look at you!" Mrs. Webber enfolded me in a tight hug. I was never much of a hugger, but over time I was being won over to it. In fact, if I'm completely honest, I'm beginning to enjoy it just a little bit, if it isn't overdone. Fortunately, Mrs. Webber knew just how long to hold a hug, releasing me before I felt suffocated. "You haven't changed a bit!" She exclaimed.

"Neither have you!" I lied in answer to her lie. Actually, she did look pretty good, a bit of gray in the hair and a bit of thickening in the hips, but really, for a woman sliding fast into her sixties, she looked great.

"So, come in the kitchen and have a cup of coffee and tell me what it is you need from me. I couldn't believe it when Gina told me you had become a private detective, of all things! Gracious, whoever would have thought Rainie Lovingston would end up working law enforcement? And your mother, why, she must be pretty unhappy with it, you working for "the Man" and all!" Mrs. Webber laughed, and I wasn't quite sure how to respond.

"I'm not a private detective, just an assistant, and really, we don't enforce the law."

"Oh honey, I know that, I'm just kidding

with you. And I'm sure your mother is very proud of you. How is she, anyway? Does she still keep those special herbs in her greenhouse? I warned her years ago, at a committee meeting for RAM, that she'd better be careful with that stuff. Not everyone in Buchanan is as enlightened as I am."

I had forgotten how much - and how fast - Mrs. Webber could talk. She was a bright enough lady, but she had a few issues when it came to focusing on a single subject.

"She grows with government permission, now."

"Oh yes, that marijuana law got passed, didn't it. Well, how nice for her." We had reached the kitchen and Mrs. Webber poured coffee into two waiting mugs. "She's such a delightful person, so generous with the food and clothing drives, it would just break my heart if she got arrested. Now, I don't understand her religious beliefs, hers are even stranger than the Presbyterians, but it doesn't matter what I understand, as long as she is at peace with God, right?"

"Right," I agreed, shaking my head when Mrs. Webber pointed at the cream and sugar.

"Well, sit down, tell me what else is going on in your life. Gina tells me you take care of old people too, is that right?"

"Yes, I do that part time."

"Well, isn't that something. You are nothing like I thought you would grow up to be, you were such a wild child, I always expected something terrible to happen whenever you and Gina were out of my sight. Don't get me wrong, I know Gina was no innocent, getting dragged in over her head, she was just as bad, or worse than you." She lightly stroked her hair. "I can thank you girls for every one of these gray hairs, I'm sure."

"I'm sorry if we gave you any sleepless nights." I smiled when I said it, but I did regret giving this nice lady such fits.

"Oh, don't worry about that, Gina has more than made up for any bad nights by giving me those two wonderful grandchildren... who in a few years will keep her up at night!" Mrs. Webber laughed cheerfully. "My only regret is she didn't have a girl! Besides, truth be told I wasn't an angel either. I had my moments, just like everyone else. It's all a part of growing up."

"I suppose it is. We learn from our mistakes, and all that."

We chatted a few more minutes, which mostly consisted of me listening to Mrs. Webber rattle off sentences like a vocal Gatling gun and me interjecting a comment here and there when she paused to reload. I remembered sitting at the dinner table with Gina's family, listening to her mother go on and on, her father just grunting or smiling now and then. At least the woman was interesting, most of the time, and she was definitely likable.

She stopped talking to pour us a second cup of coffee, and finally decided it was time to get down to business.

"So, you said you had a picture you want me to look at?"

"Yes, it's from a long time ago, but I was hoping maybe you would recognize him." I pulled the photograph out of my purse and held it out to her.

"Well, aren't you going to tell me what this is all about first?"

"I'd prefer you look at the picture first, and give me your first impression."

"Oh, I get it, so you don't give me a clue so I misidentify him." She giggled. "I watch *Law and Order*, I know the drill!"

She looked at the picture, even squinting her eyes at it, as if that would help her focus. "Hmm, no, I'm sorry, I don't know him. Handsome young man, though. This looks like he was maybe in high school at the time, you think? Why are you looking for him?"

"He has a daughter who lost touch with him years ago. She wants to find him, but she doesn't have much information to go on."

"Oh my, that's so sad. But what made

you think I might know him?"

"Because, back when I was a kid, it seemed like you knew *everyone* in Buchanan. I thought that if he grew up in town you might recognize him."

"Oh, that was a good idea; you're so clever at this detective stuff. I'm sorry I can't help."

"That's okay, Mrs. Webber. It was nice to visit with you, anyway."

"Yes, this was nice! We should get together with Gina and go out for lunch some day, just us girls!"

"I'd like that. Gina and I promised to get together for coffee soon, so I'll mention it to her then."

"Wonderful."

Mrs. Webber walked me to the door. "You know, Rainie, I know who you should show that picture to: George Aller, over at the gas station by the high school. The kids all used to hang out there when George's boy was around."

"That's a good idea, but I thought George retired."

"Oh, he did, but he still hangs around there now and then. I know he's almost always there on Friday afternoons and Saturday mornings. He doesn't trust the help on the busiest days."

"That's great, Mrs. Webber. Thanks a lot,

really. It was good seeing you."

"Good to see you, Rainie. Take care."

I backed out of the driveway with a wave and tried to decide what to do next. It was almost four o'clock; did that count as putting in a full day for B&E? I had started at eight and hadn't really taken much of a lunch, so I decided that yes, it was all good. I pointed my little Escort toward home.

## Chapter Four

I spent Thursday with Thelma, as usual, and so had no time to show the photo around. On Friday morning I went to work with Maggie, and I knocked on the door at five minutes to eight, as always with a slight feeling of trepidation. I was never sure how Maggie would greet me; she seemed to be taking a liking to me, but she had a flash temper, and she was always clear about the fact that she did not think she needed a caregiver.

"Good morning!" I greeted her cheerfully.

"Good morning." Her reply was a bit more subdued, but she did offer me a hint of a smile.

"How are you today, Maggie?"

"As good as I always am, and no more in need of you today than I was last week."

"I understand, but I thought you were going to think of some chores you wanted me to do."

"I've been thinking. I might have even come up with one," she admitted grudgingly.

"Follow me."

She led me into her bedroom and folded back the doors on a rather large closet. "I've been trying to clean out some clutter. I want to go through those boxes." She pointed at several cardboard boxes neatly stacked on a high shelf. "I was going to get them down myself, but I figured that would just piss Margaret off, so I waited for you. Do you think you can lift them down?"

"Sure. Do you have a step stool?"

"Right over there." She pointed at the corner by her bed, and I brought the ancient but sturdy looking little step ladder over. I climbed up and got a hold of the first box; it was pretty heavy, and I was glad Maggie hadn't tried it. With her brittle bones it might have literally crushed her into the floor.

I lifted it down and set it on the floor.

"Do you want them all at once or one at a time?"

"Oh, bring them all down. We can take them into the kitchen one at a time and sort through them."

I did as she asked, and toted the first box to the kitchen, where she had me set it on the kitchen table.

She opened the box and stood looking at the contents for a moment.

"You know, five years ago I had to move out of the house I shared with my husband for almost forty years. I didn't want to do it, but I just couldn't keep up with the yard and all anymore. We got rid of a lot of stuff; forty years accumulation gone over a weekend in a yard sale and donations. But I kept a few things that were too valuable to give up."

She lifted out a white box and opened it to show me the contents. It was a bridal veil, wrapped in tissue paper. "My veil. Margaret plans to wear it if she ever decides to get married. To tell you the truth, I don't think that's going to happen. She's entirely too independent to put up with a roommate, yet alone a husband. But I think it's time for her to take this home with her. Maybe she can cover a lampshade with it." Maggie smiled, but I could see the sadness in her eyes.

"You never know, maybe she'll find a man who doesn't mind her independence."

"Only if she meets someone from Mars," Maggie chuckled. "For all their claims of supporting women's rights, most American men still want a woman to take care of them."

"Most, not all." I don't know why I was defending men. Personally, I pretty much agreed with Maggie's assessment.

"Anyway, most of the things in these boxes are items I saved for the kids. I want to sort them out and get it all to them now. I hate the idea of them having to go through this stuff after I'm dead. Don't get me wrong, I don't mind if they grieve for me; hell, if I didn't think they'd miss me I'd just as soon go now and get it over with! But I also don't want them hanging around here, sobbing over my old things and lingering over their grief. I want a big Irish wake, with everyone getting drunk and telling each other stories about me. In fact, I thought about writing down some of the wilder escapades of my youth for them to read aloud just to be sure there's some laughing going on."

"Oh, that's funny!" I laughed with her. "But maybe you should just tell your kids the stories now, so you can hear them laugh."

"Hey, now that's a thought. Like the people who have a wake before they're dead, so they can hear what everyone has to say about them."

"Maybe something more festive, like a birthday party, and over cake you can tell them your stories."

"I'm liking this idea!" Maggie's eyes were sparkling. "My son always brings his family for a few days in June, right around my birthday. That would be the perfect time! Of course, some of those stories might have to wait until the grandkids are in bed." Maggie winked at me. "I wasn't always a sweet little old lady, you know."

I actually snorted a laugh at that; I had rarely seen the "sweet" side of Maggie. "I wish I could be here to hear those stories."

"Well, we'll see. If you can keep from pissing me off too bad between now and then, maybe I'll invite you."

"I'll do my best."

"Okay, but don't suck up too much. I like the fact that you keep coming back at me no matter how nasty I am. Makes me feel like I'm not all frail and hanging around death's door."

"Well, obviously you're not!"

"I know that, but this whole needing a caregiver business really threw me for a loop. That's for old, helpless people!"

"No, it's for people who maybe need a hand now and then. Like when they need heavy boxes lifted out of a closet. And yes, in your case it has to do with how your body is aging, but even I would call for help if I needed to move a fridge or something. It's just a matter of degrees."

"Oh, you're good," Maggie winked at me. "You should be a diplomat. Now, enough of this, let's get this box sorted out."

It took the rest of our time together to go through two of the boxes. Each item had a story that Maggie was eager to tell, and I was just as eager to hear. Funny, I was never into history class all that much, but I loved to hear personal histories. It was sort of like putting a puzzle together, seeing random pieces come together to create a picture of an individual. It especially amazes me to hear the "wild youth" stories of the elderly. Often, we tend to view seniors as "non-people," dried up husks with no more purpose, that perhaps never had a purpose to begin with; then you hear what they went through, and in spite of the difference in decades you realize it wasn't all that much different than your own. If you've never spent a morning just talking to someone past the age of seventy, I strongly recommend you put it on your list of things to do. It can be life changing.

We finished the second box, and now we had three neat piles on the kitchen table, one for Maggie's son, one for Margaret, and one for the grandkids. Maggie looked at the wall clock.

"Uh oh! It's twelve thirty! I kept you a half hour over!"

"Wow, I didn't even realize it. I was having fun."

"Well, fun or not, my budget won't allow for paying you overtime. You'd better not come until eight-thirty Monday morning to even it out."

"That's okay, I won't charge for the half hour. I'll consider the laughs as overtime pay."

"You'll never get anywhere in this world giving your time away like that," Maggie shook her head, but she was smiling. "But make an old lady happy, wait until 8:30 anyway. I'll save those other boxes for Monday."

"Oh good! I was afraid you'd do them without me and I'd miss out."

"You're a good sport, Rainie. I'm still not sure about this caregiver stuff, but you're okay."

"Gee, thanks, Maggie." I laughed and said my good byes. It was time to get on to my other job.

I drove straight to Buchanan, hoping Mrs. Webber's information was up to date and I would catch George Aller at his minimart. With any luck he would recognize the kid in the picture.

Aller's was on a side street, a small building with a big parking lot; many years ago, long before my time, there had been gas pumps, with service attendants who checked your oil and cleaned your windshield, but the pumps had been taken out years ago and the pyramids made from cans of motor oil had been replaced by pop machines. The big plate glass windows were nearly obscured by posters and neon signs proclaiming cigarette prices and lottery jackpots. There were several cars in the lot when I pulled in, people coming and going in a hurry. It was the lunch hour, and most of the exiting customers were carrying hot dogs and paper cups of coffee or soda. I held the door for a guy in brown coveralls who was juggling two wrapped hot dogs and two cups of coffee. He nodded his thanks and I entered the store.

It was a crowded space, with more shelving units than the place could comfortably hold, and a long counter crammed with a cash register, lottery machine and merchandise displays. A just past middle-aged woman was running the register, smiling cheerfully, offering a personal comment to each customer. I hadn't been in here much since high school, but the woman looked familiar. She might be the mother of someone I knew, or maybe the same cashier who had been here when I was in school; a part time high school job that turned into a career. I couldn't really remember.

An elderly man wearing blue coveralls and a knit cap stood near the register, sipping a cup of coffee. He nodded when I came in.

"Good afternoon, young lady!"

"Hi!" I answered cheerfully. "Are you George?"

"Hell no, he ain't George. I am." An even older man peered from behind a rack of candy bars. "Poor guy thinks he's a Walmart greeter. I ain't got the heart to tell him this ain't Walmart!"

"I know this isn't Walmart," The first

guy retorted. "There isn't anybody shopping here in their pajamas!"

"Good point," George nodded. "So what can I do for you, young lady?"

"I was talking to Mrs. Webber the other day, and she thought maybe you could help me out." I held out the photograph. "I'm asking around to see if anyone recognizes this man, and Mrs. Webber said you knew just about every kid in high school back in the day."

"I suppose I did," George agreed, "But I didn't know many of their names. I just called most of them 'damn it' or 'get out.'"

The guy in coveralls laughed. "Yeah, and see how well that worked."

"Don't I know it... here you are, still blocking my counter thirty years later!" George looked at me.

"This face does look familiar. Is this a yearbook picture?"

"I'm not sure, but that's what it looks like to me."

"Why are you trying to identify him?"

"I work for B&E Security, and a lady hired us to find him. He's her father, and she lost touch with him years ago."

"Yeah? Well, maybe the guy wants to stay out of touch, if you know what I mean."

"Maybe," I shrugged. "But our job is to find him if we can."

"How do I know you ain't a debt

collector or something?"

His questions weren't as off-putting as you might think. They made me believe that he did recognize the person in the photo, but wasn't going to give the information if I was bringing trouble. I pulled out my ID, which of course, I should have done in the first place.

"I'm a private investigator's assistant. Rainie Lovingston."

"Lovingston? Are you one of that hippie lady's kids?"

"Well, some people call my mom that..."

"*ALL* the people call your mom that," George smiled. "That's okay, though. Not like she's hurting anyone, and last year when I was down with that broken hip she delivered Meals On Wheels to me. Always stayed and chatted a few minutes, even helped me get to the table to eat. Nice lady, even if she is a little crazy. Okay, so you sure you don't mean this fella no harm?"

"I'm sure, Mr. Aller. His daughter just wants to get to know him. She has a daughter of her own now; he'd probably want to know he has a granddaughter."

"Well, maybe he does and maybe he doesn't. Not every man is a family man, if you get my drift."

"Oh boy, do I know that's true!" I agreed fervently. I had chased enough dead beat dads in the past year to know how many preferred to duck out of that responsibility. But this guy's daughter was way past the age of child support, so I knew that wasn't an issue.

"Well, I think this kid maybe used to come in here, a long time ago," George admitted. "But truth, I don't remember his name." He handed the picture to the guy in coveralls. "How about you, Henry? You used the work the counter now and then."

Henry squinted at the picture. "Nope, I don't remember him. But you know who you need to show this to, is Wheeler. He was the principal at BHS for years, and he knew every one of 'his kids.' That's what he called them... he knew which ones needed a swat upside the head and which ones just needed a sympathetic ear, you know? And it was instinct, not something he learned from some class on adolescent behavior."

"There's no swatting allowed anymore," George shook his head in disgust. "Just 'time out' or suspension."

"Yeah, and that's complete nonsense. If you sent me to a corner to 'think about my actions' I wouldn't be wasting the time regretting what I did, I'd be thinking about how not to get caught the next time!"

We all laughed at that, but then it occurred to me that it might not be all that funny; isn't that pretty much what prison did for a lot of people? Not only did being locked up give them time to make better plans, it gave them access to people with a whole lot more experience at it. Of course, even those experienced criminals must not be too good at it, or they wouldn't be locked up, right?

This wasn't the time to be debating social issues, though. I pulled my mind back to the present and turned the subject back to my problem.

"I didn't realize Mr. Wheeler was still around."

"Oh sure, still up there on Carol Lane, the gray and white house on the corner of... hm, Smith Street, ain't it?" George looked to Henry for confirmation.

"Yep. The one with the mailbox painted to look like a pile of books."

"'Course, his mind isn't quite what it used to be," George cautioned me. "He has help up there now, can't live alone anymore. But I was up there last month when the weather first broke and we spent a nice afternoon reminiscing. He might forget to put his pants on without his girl to remind him, but he still remembers the old days well enough."

"Okay, I'll go talk to him. Thanks for your help."

"For what it was worth." He handed the picture back to me. "I hope you find that young lady's father. My own dad was a pain in the neck, but I sure would have hated not knowing who he was."

"You know, you could just make up posters of that picture and post them around town," Henry suggested. "You know, one of those 'have you seen me' things? If he's from around here, someone is bound to recognize him."

"Not a bad idea, except I hate to spread the guy's personal business all over town." As if I hadn't already, just by talking to these two. Half the town would know about my search before the high school let out classes.

"Oh, that's a good point," the guy nodded, as if he wasn't planning to tell the story to the next dozen people who walked through the door for a cup of coffee or a pack of smokes.

"Well, I'd better get on this. Thanks again." I waved and went out to my car.

I drove straight to Smith Street and followed it to Carol Lane, no more than six blocks from the minimart. Sure enough, there was the house with the mailbox Henry described; the paint was fading, but it still looked like a pile of books. I wondered if Mr. Wheeler had painted it himself; the work was outstanding.

I pulled into the driveway of the old house and sat for just a moment, deciding which door to approach. There was a formal looking front door, but I noted that there was no sidewalk leading to it. The main part of the house was two stories, covered in gray asphalt shingles that were probably chock full of asbestos. The section of the house nearest the driveway looked a little newer, probably built within the last fifty years or so, and it's facade was white aluminum siding. A sidewalk led to two different doors, one that seemed to be positioned between the house and the attached garage which I guessed led to a breezeway, and another that I was hoping would be the door they actually used.

My assumption was confirmed when I got out of my car and I noticed a woman already standing in the second doorway. She was blonde and middle-aged, and in politically correct terms she was "plus-sized," just as I had been not so long ago. She was peering at me curiously, her expression not quite welcoming or hostile, as if reserving judgment on how to greet me.

This, I was sure, was the caregiver. I recognized the look, having worn it on my own face many times. Caregivers fill many roles, not the least of which is watchdog. Confused clients don't need salespeople, religious nuts or other unsavory characters disturbing them, and a good caregiver will head such types off before the client even knows they are there.

I put on my friendliest smile and approached the door.

"Hi! My name is Rainie Lovingston. Are you Mr. Wheeler's caregiver?"

"Yes." She reluctantly accepted my outstretched hand and shook it. Her grip was strong, and I got the unspoken message: don't mess with me. She did, however, offer me her name.

"I'm Melody. What can I do for you?"

I held out my B&E ID. "I'm a private investigator's assistant, and I was hoping to get just a few moment of Mr. Wheeler's time."

"Why?" Melody was now frowning a bit, and I couldn't blame her. Private detectives rarely meant good news. I figured I'd better talk fast before her protective instinct pulled into high gear and she slammed the door in my face. Caregivers can be as rabid about protecting their client's best interests as a mama bear defending her cub, even ushering family members to the door if they were particularly obnoxious. Hadn't I just rushed a man with a loaded gun a couple of weeks ago to protect Thelma?

"Look, I understand your reluctance. I really only work for B&E part time. The rest of the time I'm a caregiver, too. I don't want to do anything to upset your client."

"You're a caregiver?" She looked at me suspiciously. "Who do you work for? An agency?"

"No, I work independently. Right now I take care of a lady named Maggie Shea, but I used to take care of Bob Dreisel, Mabel Hively and Max Conan."

"Bob Dreisel? He was a teacher, wasn't he?"

"Yes, retired from IUSB."

"Frank talks about him now and then. Bob did some subbing at the high school after he retired from the college. Frank was pretty fond of him."

"So was I." I felt tears try to well up at my memories of Bob, and I blinked them away. Melody, being in tune with that sort of thing, immediately softened her stance. I hadn't intended that, but hey, whatever works.

"I heard he passed away recently. How long were you with him?"

"A little over a year. I miss him, a lot."

"I know," Melody sighed. "Every time I lose a client I think I don't ever want to go through that again, but then I get a call and I can't say no."

"I know that feeling. I took this job with B&E because I needed a little break from caregiving, but I don't want to give it up completely."

"I can't *not* do it, if you know what I mean." Melody smiled.

"I do know, exactly."

Well, what do you know. Melody and I seemed to be bonding.

"Okay, so tell me what you want with Frank."

"The case I'm working doesn't actually involve Mr. Wheeler, I'm just hoping he might be able to give me some information." I held out the picture. "I'm just trying to identify this man. It's possible he went to Buchanan High School in the eighties, and George Aller, at the Mini-Mart, thought Mr. Wheeler might remember him." It always helps to mention as many names as possible when you are investigating in a small town; it makes it seem as if you are all one, big happy family, which in a way, we were, albeit a dysfunctional one at times.

Melody looked at the picture. "Who wants him identified?"

I hesitated only a moment before answering. There is a matter of client confidentiality, but again, this is a small town. People tended to be curious. Well, nosy, really, but hey, that's just a matter of word play, right? Besides, I didn't see how there was any harm in explaining the situation again.

"We've been hired by his daughter to find him. She lost touch with him years ago, and she would like to reconnect."

"Why did she lose touch?"

"Her parents split up, and she was

adopted by her stepfather. From the sound of things, it was a bitter break up, and her mother didn't want anything to do with the man."

"Maybe she had a good reason," Melody pointed out. "Maybe the guy is an abuser."

"Maybe," I agreed. "But our client is a grown woman now, and I think she can handle it. She just wants to know who he is. She has a child of her own now, and her heritage is important to her."

Melody looked at the picture again, then back at me, considering.

"Well, I don't see how this could upset Frank. In fact, he might enjoy the visit and the chance to work his memory. He has some dementia, so he might be a little confused, but he does remember the past."

"So you'll let me ask him?"

"Sure. But if he starts to get agitated..."

"I'll leave, I promise." I assured her.

"Okay, come on in." She stepped back and held the screen door for me, and I stepped into an only slightly outdated kitchen. She led me through an archway into the older part of the house. This had probably once been the main residence of a big farm, with no indoor plumbing. The kitchen and bathroom were both in the "new" addition; she led me down a hallway past two bedrooms and into a large living room.

Mr. Wheeler was sitting in an armchair

with a blanket over his lap, his head thrown back, sound asleep. He was thin but not emaciated, as if it came naturally to him rather than as a product of old age. His hair was thick and white and neatly combed, and I noted he was wearing hearing aids as well as glasses.

"Frank?" Melody touched him gently on the shoulder and he opened his eyes. For a few seconds his expression was blank, then recognition dawned in them and he smiled.

"Is it time for lunch?"

"Not yet. I'm sorry to disturb your nap, but there's a lady here who wants to ask you a question."

"What kind of question?" Frank looked a little panicky. "My mind doesn't feel all that clear today, Melody, I don't know if I can answer a question."

"It's okay if you can't," she assured him. She held the picture out to him. "She just wants to know if you recognize this guy."

Frank took the picture but didn't look at it. Instead, he peered around Melody to look at me.

"Who are you?"

"I'm Rainie." I stepped forward and offered my hand, and he shook it gently, his own hand warm and dry. "I'm trying to identify this man, and we think he might have gone to Buchanan High School some years ago. George Aller thought you might know him."

"George? How is he? Haven't seen him in a long time."

"He's good, semi-retired but still working the station a few hours a week."

"Retired?" Frank looked confused. "He's young for that, isn't he?"

This was a product of the dementia, and required gentle prodding to orient him to the present.

"Actually, I think he's nearly eighty years old."

"Eighty? How could that be..." Frank looked at Melody, and she nodded.

"That would be about right, Frank. You're going to be eighty-five next month."

"I am...?" He looked around the room, then down at his hands, and finally shook his head. "See, I told you my head isn't good today."

"You're just a bit confused. You know it's always worse when you first wake up. Give yourself a few minutes." She held out a plastic cup with a straw. "Have a bit of water."

Frank accepted the cup and drank thirstily. He set it back on the table.

"Love cold water." He peered at me and frowned. "What is it you said you wanted? Are you the visiting nurse?"

"No sir, my name is Rainie. I'm hoping you can identify the guy in that picture."

"Picture? Oh, yes," Frank suddenly

remembered the photo in his lap and picked it up, this time taking a good look at it. "Yes... he does look familiar..."

I waited, not letting my hopes get too high. Frank stared at the picture, frowning.

"He was a decent student, but a bit of a smart aleck... his mouth got him sent to my office quite a few times. Oh, nothing serious, you understand, just a bit too big for his britches..." Frank's gaze moved away from the photo and he got that vague look on his face people get when they are lost in memories. Melody and I both stayed silent, letting him troll through the past in search of the student's name... at least, I hoped that's what he was doing, and not just trying to remember what he had for breakfast. With dementia, it's hard to know sometimes.

"So many students passed through my office," Frank said after a long pause. "Of course, only the misbehaving ones got sent to me, but I spent a lot of time in the halls and the classrooms, got to know all the students, good and bad. That's what a good principal does. You can't just sit in your office doing paperwork and meting out discipline. You have to be out there, have to know your students and faculty if you want to be sure everyone is getting the education they need. And that's what it's all about, although you wouldn't know it the way the schools are run today. All this crap about standardized testing... kids aren't standardized, never have been, never should be. They're individuals, all learning in different ways at different rates. Some are better at math, some at reading, some at everything, and the key is to know the child, to encourage their strong suits so they can feel successful, not shame them by passing out low scores on meaningless tests because they don't know what "numerator" means. Sure, everyone benefits from basic math skills, but in this day and age there are calculators that can fill in those knowledge gaps. I saw kids want to quit school in frustration over a math or English class that they just didn't understand. Doesn't make sense to treat a kid that way. It's like throwing the baby out with the bathwater..."

Frank abruptly stopped talking and looked at Melody, then at me. "I'm sorry, I think I was going on a bit. What was the question?"

"The photograph, Frank," Melody gently reminded him, pointing at the picture that he still held in his hand. "Do you remember that boy's name?"

"Oh, yes... " Frank looked at the picture again. "Sure, this is... David... no, that's not it, but it starts with D... Dan... " he frowned at the photo, then suddenly broke into a smile. "Drew! That's it! I remember because he got sent to me one time for some graffiti he scrawled on the wall of a tool shed on school property... Drew got caught drawing, get it?" He chuckled. "Drew Risner, that's his name. Smart kid."

"Drew Risner?" Melody and I looked at each other in surprise. Drew Risner was pretty well known in Buchanan. He was a doctor with a huge practice in Chicago, but he had been buying up quite a bit of property in Buchanan the past few years, trying to boost his old hometown.

Melody had one eyebrow cocked in a comically skeptical expression.

"Wow, lucky girl, to discover her long lost daddy is one of the richest men in town."

Funny, but I was thinking exactly the same thing. Melody and I seemed to be kindred spirits in more ways than one.

"Just how much do you know about this daughter?" Melody asked.

"Just what she told us. We aren't paid to investigate our clients."

"Maybe you should."

"Not my call. Besides, maybe it *is* just luck. I mean, it isn't as if she could be going after him for back child support this late in the game."

"I suppose not, but... "

"Is it about time for lunch?" Frank interrupted our speculation. He had dropped the photo, and I'm pretty sure he had already forgotten what we were discussing. "I'm pretty hungry."

"Sure, Frank, it's a little early, but if you're hungry, let's go eat." Melody patted his hand. "Just let me see Rainie to the door."

"Who?" Frank peered at me. "Were you here to see me? I'm sorry, was I sleeping?"

"Yes, I'm afraid I woke you up, but you were very helpful." I retrieved the picture before it slid to the floor. "I appreciate your time, Mr. Wheeler."

"Oh, any time, any time, young lady. You come back and see me soon."

"Enjoy your lunch, Mr. Wheeler." I also patted his hand before following Melody to the door.

"Thank you for letting me talk to him." I shook Melody's hand again.

"I'm glad he was able to help... I think."

"Don't worry, the PI will review this information and handle it accordingly. B&E has a pretty high standards and a good reputation to maintain. They aren't going to knowingly assist in any kind of scam."

"I hope not. I don't really know Drew Risner, but he's helped quite a few small businesses get a start here in town. You know, he bought that big old building on Front Street that used to be part of Clark Equipment, and he rents the office space out really cheap to encourage new businesses. He's good for the community."

I nodded. Clark Equipment had been a huge presence in Buchanan back in the day; many of the old buildings had been torn down, but it was good to see at least one of the old behemoths being put to good use. "I'll be sure to mention that to the PI when I make my report."

I smiled and waved good bye. I was pretty pleased with myself for solving this case so quickly. Maybe I should give more thought to being a full time private eye; I did seem to have a knack for it.

Then I thought of Melody and Frank, and that reminded me of Bob and so many other people I had had the pleasure to care for; no, I didn't think I was going to give up caregiving completely for a long time to come.

I started my car and looked at the clock on the dashboard. It was only two-thirty, which left me plenty of time to drive to B&E to write up my report. On the other hand, I hadn't had lunch yet, and I was only a few blocks from home. I decided to stop at home and eat before driving to Niles.

# Chapter Five

**I** was walking up to the house when I heard a rustling in the bushes. I stopped, thinking it might be a cat or a dog... but no.

"Pssst... hey, Rainie... it's me, Terry."

"Terry? What are you doing in my bushes?"

"Shh... not so loud. Can I come in the house?"

"Um..." I uttered that intelligent, space keeping syllable to give my brain time to catch up with my mouth. My first instinct, of course, was to say "sure, why not?" Terry is, after all, my brother's best friend, and to some odd degree, a friend of mine.

But Terry had to be hiding in the bushes for some reason... and it was probably something I didn't want to know about.

Nonetheless, I just sighed and nodded.

"Sure, Terry, come on in."

He didn't come out of the bushes until I had unlocked the door, then he scurried in, his shoulders hunched as if to make a smaller target of himself, and he hurriedly slammed the door shut behind him and thumbed the deadbolt closed.

"All right, Terry. What is it this time? Are you being chased by mobsters, or is it aliens?"

"What? Hey, I don't mess with no mobsters, and what would aliens want with me?" He stared at me, wide eyed. Without a hint of a smile.

"I was kidding, Terry," I explained, not too patiently. "So what *IS* the problem?"

"I think the cops might be looking for me. I needed to get off the street, and yours was the closest place. Man, I didn't think you'd ever get home, I been hiding in those bushes for hours... I thought about trying a window but I figured if you came in and I startled you, you might go all PI bad ass on me and shoot me or whatever..."

"I don't shoot people... well, very often... and I am not a bad ass!"

"Sure, okay..." Terry held up his hands, as if to calm me down. Did I sound mad? I didn't think I was... then again, I wasn't exactly overjoyed at the moment, either.

"And don't *EVER* break into my house!"

"I won't! I just said that, didn't I? Man, are you havin' a bad day or what?"

"I wasn't." I rolled my eyes. "Please, Terry, just tell me what's going on, okay?"

"Yeah, okay... so I got this new job,

working overnights over at Fapco... you know, packing parts and stuff... over on Bakertown?" I nodded, but he didn't really wait to see if I was with him. "So I got the job through one of them temp agencies... that's the only way they hire, 'cause then they don't have to pay benefits, you know? So that sucks but hey, a job's a job, right? So at the end of the shift they tell me and three other guys that the temp job is over already... we'd only been there two weeks, hardly worth the paperwork, right? So the guy I rode in with, he was pretty bummed too, so he says, hey, I gotta joint, don't have to worry 'bout no drug testing for a while, let's smoke it, right?"

Well, if it had been me I would have worried about drug testing for a new job, but I didn't bother to interrupt Terry with this sage advice. Not only would it have gone unheeded, stopping Terry in the middle of a story was like trying to catch a swarm of cockroaches. So I just nodded agreement and he went on.

"So we smoke it, and about half way through I'm like 'whoa! This is some good shit, where'd you get this stuff?' 'cause I was already way high, and he says he got it from a friend, it's medical grade marijuana, like the cancer victims smoke, and it's top quality... major buzz, you know? So I took a couple more hits but then I said, 'no more, man...

that's too much for me!' but by then I was so high... I mean, that was really some good weed, you know?"

"Not really..." I said when he paused for breath, but he wasn't much interested in my knowledge – or lack thereof – of the quality of marijuana available.

"So anyway, Frank says he don't want to go straight home to bed, why don't we stop by his place and shoot some cans... he don't like real guns, and I ain't supposed to mess with 'em since I got out of jail a while back, but he's got some BB guns, and it's kinda fun, shootin' with 'em, especially when you're high, so I says 'yeah, okay,' so we go to his place and shoot some stuff. Well, after a while I realized I was gettin' kinda hungry, and I says 'man, I got the munchies bad! I need me some Pringles potato chips!' And it had to be Pringles, you know... that's what I needed, right then and there! So my buddy Frank... Frank, he lives out by me, on Miller Road, that's why we was riding to work together... anyway, Frank says okay, we'll drive in to Bec's grocery store and get us some. You know, 'cause Bec's is out there on Front Street, we figure we won't have to come all the way in town, seeing as how buzzed we were and all."

"Makes sense." I said, unnecessarily. He was already going on.

"So I go in, and there's like a dozen

kinds of Pringles, and it takes me awhile to find the right ones... I like them bar-b-que flavored, they're nice and salty, not too hot, kind of sweet... anyway, I find those, but then I also see them little carrot cakes that comes all wrapped up, all full of raisins and that sweet icing on top... man, I love those, too! So I grabbed a couple, thinkin' Frank might want one, and I go up to the counter, and it's some lady working. Now, I ain't seen no lady working in there since them foreigners bought the place... they're Arabs or some such shit, right?"

"Actually, Indian..."

"Yeah, yeah, whatever, I know they're from some place over there..." ("over there" apparently meaning over on the other side of the ocean. I like Terry well enough, but sometimes...) "So anyway, this lady is wearing one of them wrap around thingies, kind of like a dress but not really... and she says something, but I don't quite catch it, and I say 'Huh?' and she says it again, and I still don't understand, so then I get it that her English ain't so good, right? But hey, it's early, there ain't nobody else in there at that hour... I mean, most people stop there for beer and ice, and who needs beer at that time of morning, right? So I figure those Arabs have the womenfolk work the slow hours... anyway, they're nice enough folks, I don't wanna give her a hard time, 'cause you know, she speaks better English than I speak whatever language her people speak, so I just smile and nod at whatever she said, and I go to get my money out of my pocket, but when I do, I lift up my sweatshirt and I forgot I had that BB gun tucked in my waistband..."

Uh oh.

"Terry, you didn't rob Bec's, did you?"

"No! I mean, not on purpose! It was like... an accident, right? Let me tell you... so the lady gets all scared and shakin' her head, saying 'no shoot me! no shoot me!' and I like, laughed when I realized she was scared of the BB gun, so I pull it out to show her it ain't real, and she starts crying and opens the register and starts throwing cash on the counter, and I'm like 'no, lady! No! I ain't robbing you! I just want to pay for my Pringles!' but she ain't understanding me, and she's pushing the money at me, and now she's starting this weird wailing noise, like a cop siren just winding up, you know? And I know it's about to get real loud in there, and so I threw a fiver on the counter and snatched up my Pringles and ran for the door!"

"So you still took the Pringles..."

"Yeah, yeah, I know I shoulda left the Pringles, but I really *wanted* them, man, you know? I mean, I *had* to have them things! But then this guy comes from the back room, must be her husband or somethin', and he's carrying a baseball bat! So I go flyin' out of there, and this guy is fast, he's right behind me, and I run for the car but Frank sees the guy chasin' me and freaks out and hits the gas and takes off without me! So I know I should be pissed, but hey, he was really high, and he's probably sorry now, right? So I just kept runnin', and I went across the street into the graveyard, and the guy stopped and just kept yellin' at me, shakin' the bat, so I think maybe it's some religious shit, right, that he won't run through the grave yard? I don't know, them foreigners have their ways and all... anyway, so I just kept runnin', and I come out the other side, and I figure the Arab has probably called the cops, so I needed to get outa sight, and your house was closest... so I got here and you ain't home, but I saw a cop drive by so I got in the bushes, and I was too scared to try to get to Jason's place, so I just hid out and ate my Pringles and waited for you."

    He stopped, finally, and stared at me, wide-eyed and a little breathless. I stared back for a long moment.

    "Okay. So now what?" I asked after a long silence.

    "I don't know what to do! They prob'ly got my picture on their cameras, and the cops will go to my house and I'll go to jail, but it ain't my fault, Rainie! I didn't steal nothin'! I left the money and all... I didn't do nothin' wrong! I was hopin' you might have an idea, you and Jason are so smart and all..."

"Right. I'm so smart I let you in."

"Hey, that was just human kindness, right? So anyway, what do you think I should do?"

"I don't know, Terry, this is a real mess!"

"Tell me about it! Damn, I sure don't want to go to jail, I been real careful not to do anything wrong!"

"Except get high and drive around with a gun..."

"A BB gun! And I wasn't even drivin'..."

"Okay, okay, let me think a minute!" I cut him off before he could go on another rant. What was the best thing to do? He was right, he was probably on camera, and that should show his innocence... but of course, it wouldn't. Without sound, all it would show was a very stoned guy pulling a gun out from under his shirt and waving it at the lady while she threw money on the counter. But it would show him throw his own money down and leave with just the Pringles, right? That is, if someone took the time to review the tape carefully...

"All right, I have an idea. I think you should turn yourself in..."

"No way! Huh uh, the Buchanan cops

hate me... they hate my whole family, except the rich side, they'll throw me in jail and swallow the key..."

"Hold on!" I held up a hand and made him stop. "I know one of the cops, he might listen to me. I'll explain the situation before I turn you over to him, okay?"

"Which cop?"

"Brubeck. He seems cool, and he seems to have a sense of humor."

"A sense of humor? What good is that going to do?"

I just stared at Terry. Really, he couldn't see the humor in his story? Well, maybe I wouldn't either if it was me facing jail time.

"Just trust me, Terry. You can hide out on the back porch while I talk to Officer Brubeck, and if things go bad you can run to Canada."

"Canada? What am I gonna to do there? I don't speak Canadian!"

I took a deep breath and bit my lip; I did not want to laugh at Terry, not now, in his time of need.

"We'll figure something out. Just give me a minute, okay?"

"Okay... look, you got any soda around here? I ate all them Pringles and now I got a mean case of cotton mouth..."

"I don't have any soda, just water."

"Water? No juice or nothin'?"

"Sorry, Terry, just water."

"Oh man... okay... " He looked as disappointed as if I'd told him he couldn't have a new puppy.

"You could always run over to Bec's for a pop... " I suggested with a sarcastic little smile.

"Are you crazy? I can't..." suddenly he laughed. "Oh, I get it, you're kidding, trying to lighten my mood, right? Very funny, Rainie... so, water, huh..."

"There's a pitcher in the fridge, nice and cold." I pointed toward the kitchen. "Help yourself while I make the call."

I picked up the phone, but just stood there staring at it for a few minutes. The question was, how to call Brubeck? I didn't want to make an official report, so the first thing would be to try finding his home number. I went to my computer and got on line. I preferred paper phone books, but since so many companies had started printing their own they weren't very reliable. I don't know what criteria they used for deciding whose number to print and whose to omit, but it seemed pretty random to me.

I tried a couple of white pages websites, but got no results for "Paul Brubaker, Buchanan MI." Well shoot. Nothing for it then, I would have to call the police department and try to reach him through there.

I found the number and dialed, and after only two rings a female voice answered.

"Buchanan City Police Department."

"Good morning," I said in my friendliest tone. "I was wondering if it would be possible to get a message to one of your police officers?"

"What sort of message?"

"It has to do with... police business."

"Is this Rainbow Lovingston?"

"How... oh, caller I.D. Yes, this is Rainie."

If silence could sound annoyed, the next ten seconds would definitely have echoed with it. Finally she spoke again.

"Okay, which officer and what is the message?"

"Officer Brubaker, and I would just like him to call me."

"Is this a personal matter? Because we can't pass on personal messages."

"No, like I said, it's police business."

"But not something you will tell me?"

"I would prefer to talk directly to him."

"Right. Okay, I'll pass the message on to him. He can reach you at your home number?"

"Yes, but let me leave you my cell number just in case." I rattled it off and she repeated it back.

"Thank you for calling," She said, not really sounding grateful, and hung up.

Just as I was replacing the phone on its cradle Terry came out of the kitchen, eating something that looked suspiciously like peanut butter and jelly in a bowl.

"What are you eating?" I asked.

"Peanut butter and jelly. I was really hungry, but I couldn't find any bread."

"I don't eat much bread. I didn't think I had any jelly, though."

"Well, you don't, but I found some little cups of jell-o in the cupboard, and it's just as good."

Peanut butter and jell-o. Well, I've heard of worst munchies concoctions.

"Whatever. Anyway, I left a message, but it's probably going to be awhile before Brubaker calls me back, maybe even not until tomorrow…" I cut off my explanation when the phone started to ring. Surprised, I answered it.

"Hello?"

"Miss Lovingston, I presume?"

I didn't even bother to roll my eyes at the old joke. "Officer Brubaker?"

"That would be me. I got a message you wanted to speak to me about some police matter?"

"I didn't expect to hear back so soon."

"Are you kidding? Highlight of my day, getting a heads up on police work from my favorite public menace." He sounded way too amused. 'What did you get involved in this time? Did you run someone over or thwart a bank robbery? Or maybe just disrupted another food drive…"

I blushed over that last comment. I had never been sure if the police knew it was me who had driven through the TV station parking lot like a crazed loon with Jack hanging on for dear life in the back, but I guess that answered my question. I assumed they still couldn't prove it, though, or they would have arrested me.

"I'm not involved in anything," I protested. "I'm just calling on behalf of a friend."

"Right, right… a *FRIEND*. So what sort of trouble is your *FRIEND* in?"

"You don't have to say it that way. It really isn't me this time. A friend of mine has gotten himself into a sort of situation…"

"Oh, I love situations." Brubaker laughed. I like his sense of humor, but it didn't seem he was prepared to take this seriously at all. Was I the laughing stock of the Buchanan police department or was it just Brubaker that found me so funny?

"Anyway, he stopped into Bec's to get some chips this morning…"

"Hold on! That was a friend of yours that robbed Bec's?"

"No! I mean, it is a friend of mine, and it

might look like he did that, but it was just an accident…"

"Your friend accidently robbed Bec's? Oh please, tell me how that happened. I'm all ears."

"Like I said he just stopped in to get some chips…"

"Pringles," Terry corrected me around a mouthful of peanut butter and jell-o. "They technically aren't chips."

I ignored that. "…he went up to the counter, and when he got in his pocket the lady saw this toy gun he had under his sweatshirt…"

"A toy gun? Why was he carrying it concealed?"

"I don't know… because his pockets weren't deep enough? He had it stuck in the waistband of his jeans."

"Uh huh. Why?"

"Because he and a friend were shooting BBs at targets and they got hungry, so they drove into town…"

"For chips. So he was high?"

"Geez, I don't know…" I lied. "Maybe…"

"Right. So he goes in for munchies and shows the lady a gun…"

"No! At least, not on purpose. He might not have been thinking clearly…"

"Because he was high."

"Okay, he might have been, but he wasn't driving, his friend was."

"Okay. So the lady sees the gun…"

"Right, and he tried to show her it was just a plastic toy, but she freaked out, and she couldn't understand much English, and she started screaming and throwing money at him…"

"Yeah, I know. I saw the surveillance tape."

"So did you also see that he threw her the money for the Pringles before he ran away?"

"Are you kidding me, Rainie? You really expect me to believe this story?"

"I know it's crazy, but if you knew Ter- this guy, you wouldn't be all that surprised."

Brubaker chuckled. "Just knowing it's a friend of yours makes me half believe it. Don't you ever get in any normal trouble?"

"What fun would that be?" I offered a little laugh, trying to appeal to his sense of humor.

"So what is it you want me to do?"

"Just look at the surveillance tape again. You'll see how it went down, you'll see him pay for the stuff before he leaves."

"I don't know if that will matter. Flashing a gun in a public place and all…"

"It was a *toy*, and he wasn't trying to flash it, he was just trying to buy some

Pringles!"

This time Brubaker laughed outright. "Okay, okay, as dumb as this story is, I'll take another look at the tape. In the meantime, where is the guy?"

"I don't want to tell you until you look at the tape."

"He's right there with you, isn't he?"

"I didn't say that!"

"Okay, keep him there for me, anyway. It will take me a little time to review the tape."

"Will you call me back or are you going to just show up here and arrest him?"

"So you admit he is there?"

"I meant are you going to show up and *try* to arrest him…"

"Too late, Lovingston. Anyone ever tell you you're a lousy liar?" Brubaker laughed again. "I'll call you, but don't let him go anywhere."

I glanced over at Terry, who was staring at me wide-eyed, still slurping up peanut butter and jell-o. I didn't know if I had enough goodies on hand to keep him occupied for long…

"Just give me a call, okay?"

"Right." Brubaker disconnected.

"Is he coming to arrest me?" Terry was bouncing on his toes, looking like he wanted to run, but not quite willing to part with his snack.

"No. He'll call me after he reviews the tape."

"And you believe him?" I could barely understand Terry around the sticky mouthful of peanut butter he was working on.

"Sure, why wouldn't I? Just chill out, Terry…"

"I *was* chillin' before all this crap…" he swallowed hard. "I don't know how this stuff happens to me."

"Hmm, I don't know, maybe you shouldn't be riding around high…"

"Hey, I've always done that!"

"And you're always in trouble." I pointed out.

"You think this guy is gonna help me?" He apparently decided not to debate the merits of getting high with me.

"I think so, if he can. Just relax, see what he says when he calls."

"I think I oughta go wait somewheres else… just in case, you know…"

"No! I stuck my neck out for you. Now sit, and wait until he calls back!"

"Okay! Damn, Rainie, no need to yell at me and all…"

Actually, I think Terry needed yelling at a lot. And often. But that wasn't really my style.

"I'm going to have some lunch. Are you still hungry?"

"Whatcha got?"

Hm, I guess beggars *CAN* be choosers...

"I was planning to make some chicken salad."

"How you gonna eat it with no bread?"

"With a fork. You want some or not?"

"Yeah, sure... hey, thanks Rainie. Guess I should have said that already."

"Yeah... okay, you're welcome."

Terry wolfed down chicken salad and then wandered in to watch television.

"Hey, what's wrong with your TV?" He asked.

"I don't know, why?"

"I can't find Spike or AMC or anything on it. It just keeps running through the same four channels."

"Right. The three major networks and PBS. That's all I get; I don't have cable."

"What? Is that even legal? Don't they subsidize cable for poor people or something?"

"I think that's phone service, Terry. And it isn't because I'm poor, it's because I don't care to watch much TV."

"Wow. That's pretty weird."

"I'm weird? You're the one who just accidentally robbed someone with a toy gun, and you call me weird?"

"Hey, like you said, my situation is an accident. You don't have cable on *purpose*."

I rolled my eyes and went back to the kitchen. This was going to be a long afternoon; I hoped Brubaker would call soon.

I was just brewing a pot of fresh coffee when Terry wandered through the swinging door.

"Hey, I really want to go home. Will you give me a ride?"

"No way. I promised the cops you'd wait here."

"What difference does it make if I wait here or home? I'm still hungry, and I wanna watch *Duck Hunters*."

"I could order pizza..."

"Nah, I got pizza at home. And I can watch my show. It's really funny, about these rich red necks that..."

"Okay, enough, Terry," I cut him off. Just hearing about the crap that passed for entertainment on TV these days made me feel like my IQ was dropping. "If I take you home, do you promise to stay there and wait for me to call?"

Okay, I know I was giving in too easy, but the truth is Terry was already driving me crazy. What if Brubaker didn't call for a whole day? What if I had to keep him here overnight? I couldn't imagine dealing with Terry before my morning coffee.

"I promise, Rainie!" He held up two fingers, a partial Boy Scout salute. "Scout's honor."

"I don't think you were ever a Boy Scout."

"Well, I wasn't, really, but I used to date a girl that had a cousin that was, and I was gonna beat him up but I didn't, so that makes me honorable, right?"

"Right…" I learned long ago not to argue with Terry's logic. It has an algorithm all its own. "No messing around here, Terry. I put my reputation on the line for you, and I really don't need the Buchanan police pissed off at me."

"I think they already think you're kind of a trouble maker," Terry offered helpfully. "I hear talk now and then…"

"Yeah, yeah, I know. I just don't want to make it any worse, okay? Officer Brubaker doesn't seem to hate me too much, and I'd like to keep it that way."

"I swear, Rainie, I just want to go home and eat and watch TV." He sniffed his armpits. "And maybe take a shower."

Wow, I *REALLY* didn't want Terry taking a shower here. That sealed the deal.

"Okay, let's go."

Terry once again pulled his hood over his head and scurried out to my car. He got in and slumped low in the seat. I know he was trying to be sure he wasn't seen by the police, but frankly he looked just like a guy trying to hide from the police.

I didn't bother to point that out to him, just got in and drove him home.

I went back home and tended to George, then went in and took a shower, relieved that I had avoided having to share this very personal space with Terry.

I was just drying my hair when Brubaker called.

"Miss Lovingston? Brubaker here."

"Hello. Did you review the tapes?"

"We did. We're just leaving the station. We'll be at your house in a few minutes."

"We?"

But it was too late. He had already disconnected.

I hurriedly finished drying my hair, barely completing the task before my doorbell rang. I went to answer it, and had to suppress a groan when I saw who made up the "we." The police chief himself, not one of my biggest fans.

"Um… hi…" I said, using my usual talent of sparkling conversation in uncomfortable circumstances.

"Miss Lovingston," Officer Brubaker smiled, looking friendly enough. "You know Chief Harding?"

"We've met," I managed. The chief smirked at me.

"I figured I'd better see to this matter personally. The last time I didn't give one of your problems enough attention you blew up a building in my town."

"What? I never…" I was blushing and stammering. There was no way he could have known I had been in that abandoned apartment… then again, this was a small town, and I couldn't be sure no one had seen me and Jack walk away after the explosion. It was quite possible there had been enough rumors for the police to put two and two together, but not enough evidence to actually make four.

Chief Harding shook his head. "Don't worry, I don't plan to arrest you for it. Seems you did us a favor in the long run, anyway, getting rid of a meth lab and the cook all at once. Saved us the cost of a trial and got that eyesore apartment building rebuilt all in one shot. Pretty good work, really."

"I… I don't know what you mean…"

"Okay, so where's our armed robber."

"So you are here to arrest him?"

"Well, we'd like to talk to him," Brubaker said. "Where is he?"

"At home."

"Home? Miss Lovingston, you promised you'd keep him here."

"I know, but he was eating me out of house and home. I took him home so he could devastate his own groceries."

"So he's long gone." Chief Harding looked disgusted.

"No, I told you, he's at home."

"And you really think he stayed there?"

"Yeah, I really do. But you haven't told me. Are you going to arrest him?"

"Truth be told, the tape pretty much confirms his ridiculous story. And we went back and spoke to the lady at Bec's. With her brother interpreting, we were able to explain it all to her, and she actually agrees that might be what happened. And the brother says they've been having enough trouble fitting in around here without prosecuting a stoner, so no, we aren't going to arrest him, provided he doesn't have a record of this kind of thing. On the other hand, I think he at least needs a serious talking to, don't you?"

"Oh yeah, I'm with you there."

"So, give us his name and address. We'll run a check on him and then go talk to him."

"Okay, but maybe I should go with you to his house."

"Why? You think he's dangerous? Has he got a real gun, you think he'll open fire on us?"

"No! I just think Terry… well, he doesn't always think things through."

"No kidding? I never would have guessed that." The chief gave me his familiar smirk. I wonder if he ever smiles or grins, or if that sarcastic twist of his lips is the closest he can come to showing amusement. On the other hand, he wasn't going to arrest Terry, so he must have some sense of humor.

It took about fifteen minutes to drive out to Terry's house just northwest of town. I might have done it faster if it weren't for the police car following me. For the time being the cops seems more or less kindly disposed toward me; I thought that perhaps barreling down the country roads at top speed might make them less friendly.

I had only been to Terry's house once, to pick up Jason. I remembered that it was a small place on about thirty acres of wooded property. There was no lawn to speak of; the house just sort of sat in a little clearing. I suspected it had been built as a hunting cabin, but somewhere along the line Terry had taken it over as a full time residence.

I pulled into Terry's driveway, a rather long gravel trail that passed through the woods. Half way down it I was greeted by a very large barking German Shepherd. Huh, I had forgotten all about Tiny, the stolen guard dog. You would think I would remember something like that, since I had been in on the heist. I proceeded to the house, Tiny loping along beside me, barking in a way that might have been joyful or vicious, I wasn't sure. He had seemed friendly enough when he was riding in the getaway car with me, but now he was protecting his territory.

Suddenly his ears pointed forward, and he forgot about me. He raced ahead and the front door opened just long enough for him to disappear inside. Good enough; at least I knew Terry was home.

I thought Terry would come out to greet me, but the front door remained closed. I got out of my car and went up on the front porch. I knocked hard on the door and waited. After a few minutes I knocked again.

"Terry! It's me, Rainie!"

There was still no answer. By now Brubaker and Chief Harding had come up on the porch with me.

"Terry, I saw you let Tiny in, I know you're home. They aren't here to arrest you. Come on, open up!"

"Terry isn't here!" A shaky falsetto voice called from inside. "I'm his sister. He'll be back... later."

I laughed outright at the ridiculous attempt to disguise his voice. "Terry, come on! That's the worst try ever. Open the door!"

Finally I heard the lock turn, and Terry came out, Tiny at his side. The dog looked mistrustfully at the police officers, but wagged his tail at me. Apparently he remembered me aiding and abetting his getaway, and I was an accepted member of his gang. Or pack. Whatever.

"Well, that's a fine looking animal!" Chief Harding exclaimed. "Don't see many German Shepherds around anymore." The chief held his hand out. "Come 'ere, boy... that's it... " Tiny went right to him and the chief scratched his ears. "Funny thing, a couple of weeks ago I was having coffee out at the Homeplate... you know it, that restaurant by Martins in Niles?" He was looking at Terry, and Terry nodded. "Yeah? Anyway, I was having coffee with Bert Thompson, the county deputy... you might know him?"

"I've met him... " Terry was hesitant, not sure where this was going.

"Right, so Bert and I were talking about this and that, unsolved crimes and whatnot, and he mentioned that Tony Hacket, the guy that owns the tow service the county uses, just had a dog like this stolen. Someone came up and cut the fence and took the dog right out of the lot. Brazen, wouldn't you say?"

"What's brazen?" Terry asked. He was looking a little jumpy about the chief's story, and I didn't blame him. Here he was, maybe about to get away with "accidentally" robbing Bec's, but instead he was going to get busted for stealing the dog!

"That means bold," the chief explained. He ran a hand over Tiny's back and down his side. "Of course, I'm not trying to say this is the same dog. Bert says Tony's dog was so thin he'd complained twice to Tony about not caring for him properly, threatened to call the humane society on him if he didn't make it right." The Chief patted Tiny on the side. "Can't be this dog. He feels pretty well fed to me."

"I take good care of him," Terry said.

"I can see that. But you know, you want to be careful not to let him run off the property and get lost. Unless you have one of them microchips on him. Some people do that nowadays. They stick a tiny microchip under the dogs skin, has the real owners name and address on it. If the pound or whatever picks the dog up, they can use this little wand to read the chip. Pretty sure Tony had one on his dog, okay?"

"Okay..." Terry was staring at the chief, wide-eyed, not sure if he was about to be arrested or not.

"Okay, just letting you know. Keep a good eye on him, okay? I wouldn't want him picked up by the humane society. He looks like a fine dog, wouldn't want you to lose him."

"Thank you... I mean, really... that's good of you... "

"I can't stand to see an animal mistreated is all. So, down to business. We need to talk about this Bec's robbery."

"It wasn't no robbery!" Terry protested.

"I swear, it was all an accident!"

"I want you to tell me the whole story, son. Don't leave anything out."

"But..." Terry looked to me; his expression of fear was almost comical.

"Just tell them, Terry. *ALL* of it."

"Well, okay... but... I mean... I was doin' some *MAYBE* illegal stuff... I just didn't rob nobody... "

"Let's hear it."

So Terry told the story again, and I knelt down to play with Tiny so I wouldn't burst out laughing. I couldn't help it; Terry was so animated when he told a story, so ridiculously serious...

Brubaker and the chief listened without laughing, although I glanced up to see the humor in Brubaker's eyes, and Chief Harding's smirk was back.

"So I just ran and ran!" Terry finished his tale. "I didn't know what else to do!"

The chief shook his head. "That's got to be about the dumbest story I ever heard."

"But it ain't just a story! It's true, every word!"

"Yeah, that's what worries me the most. I almost think I should lock you up for stupidity... for your own safety!"

"What? No, please!" Terry started to back toward the door, but the chief held up a hand.

"I said I almost think so. I don't think it's really necessary, and besides, if I do, who's going to feed Tiny?"

"Yeah, he really depends on me!" Terry agreed eagerly.

"Right. So what we're going to do is, you're going to ride with me and Officer Brubaker up to Bec's, and you're going to apologize to that poor woman you terrorized. And if I ever catch you riding around my town stoned again, I'll throw you in jail quicker than you can wink and I'll take Tiny home myself!"

"Oh, I promise you'll never catch me!"

Brubaker and I burst out laughing, and Terry looked at me questioningly; he obviously didn't realize what he just said. Chief Harding even cracked a tiny smile.

"All right, get Tiny in the house and come on."

"Okay, let me get my keys... " Terry stopped half way into the house. "You promise you'll bring me right back?"

"Get moving, boy!" The chief roared, and Terry scampered into the house.

The chief turned to me. "Now, I don't want you thinking I'm all soft on crime because of this."

"Of course not," I agreed.

"Because I run a good department, and I don't tolerate crime in my town, you hear? Just because you took out that cop shooter and cleared up that meth mess, that doesn't give you a free ride to run rampant around Buchanan."

"I would never dream that it did."

"Good. Well, you just give us a call any time one of your friends accidentally robs a bank or something."

"I will. Thank you, Chief Harding."

I turned to go, but I couldn't help noticing his smirk was maybe a little bit friendlier than it had been in the past. Huh, maybe I was winning him over with my natural charm.

I didn't think I should bank on it, though.

# Chapter Six

At last, it was Saturday.

Even better, it was poker night. We played once a month, Mason, Riley, Jeff, Eddie (when he was in town, which he always tried to be) and lately, Jack. We played for low stakes, a dollar limit on the raises, since nearly everyone had mortgages to pay. I loved playing, win or lose; I think a lot of the appeal was the social aspect, the banter and trash talk with the guys.

For a change, I was almost happy to see it raining when I woke up; my house was in need of a good cleaning, and the rain made me more inclined to stay home.

Here's the thing about me and housework. One thing I've learned from my clients is that when I am in my final days looking back on life, I don't want my fondest memory to be of how many hours I spent keeping my house clean. On the other hand, I like things neat and organized, and I certainly don't want to live in filth. So I keep the cooking to a bare minimum and pick things up as I go;

once a week I run through and give everything a quick clean. And every month or so I do a really good job, vacuuming under the furniture, mopping the tile floors, scrubbing the tub and sinks, and all those other crappy jobs that must be done if one can't afford a maid.

I sat on the porch for a smoke with my second cup of coffee, thinking it was really time to give them up. I wondered if I could do it cold turkey? I looked at the pack: three cigarettes left. I'm not a heavy smoker, but I do love the habit. Still... I decided not to buy another pack, just to see if I could do it.

I poured a third cup of coffee and dug into the housework, and four hours later I stood in my freshly vacuumed living room looking at George's clean cage with a sense of satisfaction. I may not love housework, but I do appreciate a job well done.

"It's still raining," I told George, but he was too busy chomping on a salad of assorted fruits and veggies to answer me. He was out on his basking shelf, absorbing some artificial sunshine from his lamp while I tore his cage apart and cleaned it. "I think I'll run over to Harding's and pick up a few groceries for tonight, and then come back and read a book for a while."

George finally looked over at me, a piece of Romaine lettuce dangling from his scaly jaw.

"I'll only be gone a few minutes, so I'm going to leave you out. Don't go anywhere, okay?"

He just went back to chomping his food, not making any promises, but I decided to trust him anyway. All in all he's a pretty well-behaved iguana.

Mason and Jeff arrived right after seven o'clock, bearing trays of food. Mason brought a big veggie tray with his wife's homemade horseradish dip, and Jeff brought chips and fresh salsa. I could always count on them to bring goodies to poker, now that they were married.

"Thank your wives for me," I told them. "It's good of them to contribute to something they aren't even attending."

"I don't know about Mason," Jeff admitted with a smile, "But I'm pretty sure Julie likes it when I get out of the house for a night. I think she spends the evening doing stuff with her face... you know, mud packs or some such thing."

"Pam never seems unhappy to see me go," Mason grinned. "I assume she's not sneaking some other guy in after the kids are asleep, so my guess is she does that same facial stuff. I don't know why she bothers; she always looks great to me."

"Yeah? Well maybe she always looks great + she does the mud thing."

"Ha! Good point. Guess I won't rock the boat."

"Do you do that kind of thing, Rainie?" Jeff asked, popping a chip into his mouth.

"Nope. Never got the knack for it."

Riley came in through the back door, toting a six pack of import beer. "What are we standing around for?" He asked with a grin. "Are we playing cards, or having a coffee klatch?"

"No coffee for me," Mason raised his own beer in a mock toast. "How's it going?"

"Not bad." Riley put his six pack in the fridge, keeping one out. He reached for the opener I kept hanging under the cabinet. "How you doing, Jeff? I heard you were looking for a new job."

"Nah, I've just been scouting around, seeing if there might be some greener pastures out there. How'd you hear that?"

"I was installing a new alarm over at WorkOne and saw your name on some paperwork."

"You're nosing around on the desks?"

"Hell no! I just happened to see your name on a sticky note. I didn't read the paperwork it was attached to."

"Good to know," Jeff looked relieved. "I really don't want the bosses to know I'm looking around."

"Ah, won't hurt them to know. Good for them to stay on their toes, remind them to treat you right or you'll go work somewhere else."

"Or it makes them worry and they hire someone to preempt you leaving them in the lurch."

"Yeah, that can happen. So what? You find another job."

That was Riley for you. Didn't matter how bad the economy was or how short in supply jobs happened to be; it never even occurred to him he couldn't find a decent job whenever he wanted one. I was really fond of Riley, but sometimes his attitude of superiority rankled; he tended to think he was smarter and better than everyone else, and that therefore most rules didn't apply to him. He never outright said it, but you got the impression he thought rules were for the general masses who simply weren't intelligent enough to make logical decisions for themselves.

Jack came in a few minutes later, looking sexy as always in loose jeans and tight t shirt. I wondered if I would always get that little flutter in my tummy when he walked into a room.

"Ready to play some cards?" He greeted us.

"We might as well. I'm not sure where Eddie is."

"He had something going in Sturgis, but he said he'd be here," Jack said.

"Cool. Okay, let's get started, we'll deal him in when he gets here."

We played for almost an hour before Eddie finally showed up, sporting a freshly blooming black eye and a six pack of beer.

"Sorry I'm late," he smiled on his way past to put his beer in the fridge.

"What happened to you?" Jeff asked. "You piss off someone's husband?"

"I wish," Eddie laughed. "Nope, I pissed off someone's wife. I hate it when women like to punch; it's no fair when you can't hit them back."

"How did you piss her off?"

"I was taking her husband into custody for jumping bail. She didn't want me to do that."

"So she punched you?" I would never understand people. "Was she crazy?" Eddie is a big guy, and although not as bad as Jack, still pretty scary looking.

"I think she was, a little," Eddie laughed.

"I can't believe you let her connect that swing," Jack shook his head and clicked his tongue. "You're slipping."

"I know, kind of pissed me off, but I wasn't expecting it. She was just a little thing, maybe five feet tall. She was just standing there, asking me why I was taking him, and I was busy getting cuffs on him, then all of a sudden she hauled off and slugged me."

"You're lucky she didn't have a knife," Jack pointed out, his tone serious.

"Yeah, I know," Eddie sighed. "Truth is, I've been thinking it might be time for a little R&R. I've been hitting it pretty hard for a while."

"Sounds good," Jack agreed. "Maybe hit some quiet South American beach, find yourself a little chica to keep you company, drink some liquor and forget the world for awhile."

I couldn't help a little stab of jealousy at the thought of Jack on some beach with a "little chica." I suppose that is his idea of a vacation; what did I expect?

"I might do that," Eddie nodded. "I'll talk to Harry Monday morning, see about clearing my schedule for a couple of weeks in June... that is, if we have your business finished up by then."

"We will," Jack said confidently. "His" business, of course, was the little matter of someone trying to kill him. I hope his confidence isn't misplaced. I was trying hard not to dwell on the possibility of someone trying to get me; and I hate the rush of fear that brought.

"Hey, let's play some cards," I suggested, wanting to change the subject.

Poker night was for lighthearted banter, not discussions of assassination attempts and burn out.

We took a break at nine o'clock and stepped out to the backyard for a smoke. The rain had passed, and it felt warmer than it had all day. I pulled out my rumpled back of cigarettes and lit my second-to-last smoke. Already I was beginning to feel that familiar panic brought on by the addiction center in my brain: "*You're almost out! You'd better get more! NOW!*" it whispered at me, then shouted when I stuck the last smoke in my pocket and didn't run straight for the corner store. Huh. Maybe this quitting was going to be harder than I thought.

We were all chatting about not much of anything, but I noticed Riley was standing a little off to the side, looking at his bottle of beer.

"Something wrong?" I asked him.

"Huh?" he looked up as if I'd startled him.

"You're pretty quiet. Is something the matter?"

"Not really... I mean... maybe..." he rubbed his forehead. "I'm not feeling so good. This beer tastes like crap."

"Uh oh," I peered at him, but there wasn't much to see in the dark. "There's a nasty flu going around."

"Oh man, I hope that's not it." He poured his beer out into a bush. "I sure don't want any more of that, though."

"Well, hey, no offense, but if you're sick..."

"Yeah, yeah, I know, I shouldn't be here. Whatever; my head hurts pretty bad anyway. I think I'll head home." He raised his voice and called good night to the others. "I've got a headache, I'm heading out. See you all next month."

"Take it easy, Riley."

I watched him go, wondering if he was really feeling under the weather or just faking it. I remembered that last month he'd gotten a phone call and took off early. Rumor had it he was dating a married woman, and there was no doubt he'd been pretty secretive the past few months. I hadn't noticed him on his phone, but he easily could have gotten a text without me noticing.

Oh well, in the long run it was none of my business. We all finished our smokes and went back in to play cards.

I woke up Monday morning feeling cranky and out of sorts. I had smoked my last cigarette with my morning coffee on Sunday, and somehow resisted buying more all day, but the urge was on me bad. I was thinking maybe I'd pick up a pack on the way to Maggie's. I mean, I don't smoke all that much, so what the heck? It couldn't be hurting me that bad...

I turned on the news to distract myself. A fatal car accident on US 12. A stabbing in South Bend. A fifteen year old being tried for the murder of his grandfather. I was just about to click it off, regretting my decision to turn it on in the first place, when I heard them mention Buchanan. "The story, right after this."

I waited impatiently through the commercials, and finally they came back, their smiles all too bright and white for six o'clock in the morning.

"The Buchanan police department is issuing a warning to its citizens today. Last week there were three reports of a man attacking women outside their homes. There were no reported injuries beyond minor bruising, but the man held the women down and cut off large sections of their hair before releasing them and running off." A sketch appeared on the TV screen, with a phone number underneath. "This is a composite drawing of the suspect, who is reported to be approximately six feet, two inches tall and around two hundred and fifty pounds. The police urge women to be alert when they are outside, and to report any sightings of this man."

The picture was replaced by a graphic of the weather and they went on to other topics. So, the guy who tackled me wasn't out to kill me after all, and I had just spent several nervous days for nothing. Not that I would want to be tackled and given a forced haircut, you understand, but that was a far cry from being made dead! I was a little ticked off at Jack for getting me all worked up over nothing. I mean, it never had made sense to me that the guy wanting to kill *him* would come after me.

I clicked off the TV and went for a refill on my coffee. I was restless, and felt as if there was something I should be doing...

Then it occurred to me, I would normally go sit on the front porch with my second cup of coffee to smoke a cigarette. Well, what the heck, even if I wasn't smoking, there was no reason I couldn't sit on the porch and enjoy the morning. I could see the sun peeking through the east windows; it promised to be another beautiful day.

I took my coffee outside and settled into my chair as if I wasn't ready to chew off my own arm if I didn't get a nicotine fix soon. I gulped my coffee, trying to distract myself with its heat, but my mind was completely fixated on having a cigarette.

"Knock it off!" I ordered myself. Which had about as much effect as ordering a fish not to swim or a Chihuahua not to yap. Simply wasn't going to happen.

I was about to give it up as a lost cause when a black truck pulled up in front of the house. There was no mistaking that glossy paintjob: Jack. What in the world was he doing here so early in the morning?

"Hey." He greeted me, not really enlightening me to his purpose at all.

"What are you doing here?" I cut to the chase.

"Good morning to you, too. Still off the smokes?"

"Yeah, why?" I snapped.

He grinned. "Just curious."

"I doubt you stopped by this early in the morning just to check up on my bad habits. What's up?" I tried to lighten my tone. I guess maybe I had sounded a little bitchy. I hoped it was just a withdrawal symptom; I would hate to think that the nicotine had been suppressing an inner bitchiness all these years that would now be unleashed on an unsuspecting world.

"Did you watch the news this morning?"

"As a matter of fact, I did!" Now that he reminded me, I was pissed off all over again. I was just about to let him have it when he raised a hand to forestall me.

"I know what you're thinking: I overreacted, and since that guy wasn't one of the ones after me, you've been worried about nothing."

"Well... yeah!" Darn it. It wasn't nearly as satisfying to complain when *he* was the one saying the words.

"That's why I'm here. Just because that guy wasn't one of them, doesn't mean you aren't still in danger. I want you to keep up your guard."

"This is ridiculous!" The porch wasn't nearly so pleasant without a smoke, so I headed inside, Jack close behind me. "You're the target, not me. I'm not going to walk around looking over my shoulder all the time. I'll get a crick in my neck."

"You can't laugh this off, Rainie. I'm serious..."

"And so am I! Look, why don't you just find these guys already so we can all get on with our lives?"

"Huh. Why didn't I think of that?"

My reply was interrupted by my ringing cell phone; I could hear it, but I had to look around to find it. By the time I did it stopped ringing. I checked the caller ID. "Huh, that was Riley. He hasn't called much lately, I wonder what he wants?" I was about to tap the button to call back when the phone rang again: Riley.

"Wow, he really wants to talk to me." I touched the green button to answer him.

"Hey, Riley! What's…"

"Rainie, listen! Remember what we

talked about?"

"What?"

Riley sounded agitated, almost frantic. "You remember, last spring… oh hell, better not talk on the phone. You at home?"

"Yeah, but… "

"I'll come over." And he disconnected.

"What the hell?" I was staring at my phone as if it would tell me what was going on.

"Something up?" Jack wanted to know.

"I'm not sure. Riley sounded kind of weird."

"Weird? That covers a lot. How weird?"

"He was upset, almost in a panic. He was asking if I remembered something we talked about last spring. How should I know? We talk about a lot of things, and last spring was a long time ago." I fell silent, searching my memory. A lot had happened last spring. I'd taken the job with B&E, I'd been shot, I had uncovered a murder ring… I couldn't remember any specific conversations with Riley, though.

"I love a mystery." Jack grinned, not taking the situation seriously at all. Sometimes I think he thought all of my friends - except Eddie, of course - were just a bit silly.

I ignored his comment and went into the kitchen to fill George's dish. Just as I was placing it there was a knock at the door.

I have a bad habit of opening my door

when someone knocks without checking first to see who it is, a practice I should follow even if I *am* expecting someone.

There is the obvious reason why this is a bad practice: it might be a bad guy, bent on robbery, rape and or murder.

There are also the secondary reasons: it might be a pair of well-dressed young men carrying bibles or trying to sell you a vacuum cleaner.

And then there is a third reason, which is what I found when I opened the door: the cops!

Actually, it was one cop, but the lack of plurality didn't make the situation any better.

"Miss Lovingston?" The guy was holding out a leather case with his badge clearly displayed. He was wearing a cheap suit that the Mormon kids would have been ashamed to be seen in, and his hair looked as if he'd cut it himself that very morning - perhaps without benefit of a mirror. It might have been considered stylish by some, but I personally would have slapped my stylist if she let me leave the salon looking like that.

But, bad suit and haircut or not, he was still a cop. I figured I'd better be polite and keep my fashion opinions to myself until I found out what he wanted.

"That's me!" I answered brightly.

"I'm Detective Williams, of the Niles

PD. I wondered if I might come in for a minute?" He smiled, and it was actually a pretty good smile. "I just need to ask you a couple of questions."

I hesitated, but I'm not sure why. My days of having suspicious houseplants growing among the philodendrons were long over; I had absolutely nothing to hide, at least in my living room. I guess it's just an instinct instilled in me at my mother's knee to always be suspicious of authority. It was as if just his presence in my home could infuse me with guilt.

Besides, my mind was racing a mile a minute, trying to think of what I'd been doing the last couple of weeks. Had I done anything that could get me arrested? Had they finally figured out that I was the one that drove the truck through the food drive?

Ridiculous, of course. That had happened months ago, and besides, they wouldn't send a detective to arrest me for that… would they?

His smile was fading, and I realized I was staring at him opened mouthed, and had been for a bit too long. I finally nodded and stepped back.

"Sure, come on in." I flicked a glance toward Jack. He was leaning on George's cage, looking amused.

"So what questions?" I managed to

regain my cool once I closed the door and turned to face him.

"Miss Lovingston, do you know a man named Riley Whitcomb?"

"Riley? Of course, why?" I felt a little tickle of misgiving at the back of my brain.

"Have you seen him recently?"

Uh oh! I was suddenly remembering a strange conversation I'd had with Riley some time back. In fact, probably in the spring. He'd asked me to promise that if the cops ever asked me if I knew where he'd been on a particular night that I'd say he'd been at my house, playing cards. He said at the time that everyone just needed to know they had an alibi… just in case. I had teased him at the time, asking if he had plans to kill someone. He had seemed serious, but at the time he'd been drinking, and I thought he was only kidding.

But here was Detective Williams.

I blinked, realizing I'd been doing that thousand yard stare again, and forced a laugh. "Well, I haven't seen him *today*. How recent are you talking?"

"Was he here Saturday night?"

"Saturday night was poker night. We have a regular group that gets together the second Saturday of every month. Just penny ante, you know, no big stakes. We use to play the first Saturday, but we were always getting interrupted by holidays…" I was rambling and

I cut myself off.

"Miss Lovingston, the question is, was Riley Whitcomb here?"

"I can't imagine anything that would keep Riley away from a poker game." There, I hadn't actually lied, had I? I mean, he had been here, at least for a little while. I couldn't imagine what had caused him to leave early... or at least, I didn't want to imagine it.

Jack, still looking amused, decided to jump in. "It's no wonder Riley loves poker, he's got the luck of a leprechaun. Remember that seven card stud game, I had a straight to the jack and he managed to pull a flush! Good pot, too." Oh, how slick. He wasn't lying, either. That *had* happened, just not at last week's game.

"And you are?" I was relieved that Detective William's attention had shifted to Jack.

"Jack Jones. I was here for the poker game Saturday night."

"Okay, and how late did the game go?"

"We always knock off at one a.m." I told him. "Mason has to get up for eight o'clock Mass." There, throw in the fact that I had virtuous friends. We weren't just a bunch of heathen rabble, we could be trusted. "Why are you asking about Riley?"

"I'm afraid this is part of an ongoing investigation. I'm not at liberty to say."

Wow, that line sounded like it came straight off a TV cop show, but he delivered it with a straight face.

"Riley's a great guy. Whatever he's been accused of it's probably bogus."

"I didn't say he was accused of anything."

"Well, why else are you checking his alibi? That is what you're doing, isn't it?"

"This is part of an ongoing investigation. I'm not at liberty to say."

Gee, he had that line down pat.

"How long have you known Mr. Whitcomb?"

"Pretty much all my life. We grew up together."

"So you're close friends?"

"Yes, I'd say so."

"So you might lie for him, right?"

"No! I never lie. I'm no good at it." Which was true. Usually. And if he didn't quit looking at me and asking questions, I was going to start blushing and stammering and before I knew it I'd be hauled away in handcuffs...

"It's true," Jack jumped back into the conversation and took the detective's attention away from me. "Rainie and I work together, and I can vouch for the fact that she's a terrible liar."

"I see." Detective Williams frowned,

processing this information. "And what sort of work is that?"

"We're private detectives."

"Actually, I'm only an assistant," I offered helpfully. "I'm still learning the ropes. Usually I provide home care for the elderly. Not much lying necessary there."

"Okay... " Detective Williams said slowly. We had definitely taken the conversation away from the direction he had intended, but the guy wasn't stupid. He was aware we'd done so, but I don't think he had quite decided why.

"Well, thank you for your time Miss Lovingston, Mr. Jones. I'll be in touch if there's anything else I need to ask."

Oh goody.

I closed the door behind him and leaned against it, my heart in my throat.

"Oh my god! What do you suppose Riley did?"

"Hey, I thought you said Riley's a great guy…"

"Yeah, well he is! But that doesn't change the fact that I have no idea where he was or what he was doing after about nine o'clock Saturday night."

"That's not what you led the cop to believe." Jack grinned.

"I didn't really lie! I can't help what the detective assumed."

"Yeah, that was pretty smooth." Jack narrowed his eyes. "I think I'd better pay closer attention to what you're telling me in the future. I hadn't realized what an accomplished liar... or should I say, evader of the truth... you've become."

"I'm learning from the master." I performed a mock formal bow in his direction and he laughed.

"You will someday take the pebble from my palm, grasshopper!"

"What?"

"Kung Fu, the TV show? With David Carradine?"

I just shook my head, and he sighed.

"Never mind."

"The thing that worries me most is that Riley set up an alibi with me months ago."

"He set up an alibi for last Saturday?"

"He didn't give me an exact date." I went on to explain. "He pulled me aside one night, and he'd been drinking a little. He asked me, if the cops ever came by asking, if I would tell them that he had been here, playing cards. He said he wasn't planning anything, just that every guy should have an alibi they could rely on, in case 'something came up.' I agreed to it, but I kind of thought he was just kidding."

"That's a little weird, Rainie."

"I know... it's freaking me out a little."

"Hey, Rainie!" I jumped, startled by the

new voice. It was Riley, peeking around my kitchen door. "Did you lock the front door?"

"No, why would I?"

"So that cop doesn't come back in!" Riley was clinging to the door frame, only half of his face showing, as if he were ready to cut and run at the slightest provocation.

"He's not going to just bust in…"

"Rainie, please!"

Okay, this was getting weirder and weirder. I moved over and flipped the deadbolt on the front door. Riley, looking only slightly less feral, stepped into the living room. He didn't look good. He was pale and sweaty, his eyes a bit glassy. He was wearing a pair of wrinkled sweats and a worn t shirt, his hair uncombed and his feet stuffed into a pair of loafers with no socks. He would have looked ridiculous if he hadn't instead looked pathetic.

"I ran over as quick as I could, but that damned cop car was already here. I've been waiting outside for him to leave. What did you tell him?" He flicked a nervous glance at Jack, who offered an amused grin.

"What should I have told him? What's going on, Riley?"

"I think… wait, what did you tell him? Did he ask if I was here Saturday night?"

"Yeah, he did, and I implied that you were."

"Implied? What does that mean?" He

tossed another look at Jack. "You were here Saturday night, right?" His voice had risen in pitch, and for a minute I thought he might puke on my carpet.

"Yep, I was here," Jack nodded. "I backed Rainie's story... such as it was. Now I think we deserve an explanation of why we almost lied to the cops."

"Almost? Come on, what did you say?" Riley looked back to me, pleading for details.

I gave him a quick rundown of our conversation with Detective Williams. The whole time Riley was shifting back and forth from foot to foot, like a kid who needed to pee.

"Okay, okay... that's okay..." Riley wiped sweat off his forehead with his arm and for a moment stared off into the distance.

"Are you going to tell me what's going on or do I have to smack you upside the head?"

"Huh?" Riley looked back at me as if he'd forgotten I was there.

"Where did you go Saturday night? What did you do?"

"I didn't do anything. I went home to bed... I've got the flu." That seemed plausible enough. He looked like he might be suffering from Typhoid.

"So why did we need to say you were here?"

"Because I was home alone, sick in bed.

There's no way to prove where I was!"

"And why do you need to prove it?" I felt like I was pulling the information from him in tiny, sticky increments, like removing hair from a piece of taffy.

Riley coughed into his sleeve and had to grab the back of the couch with his other hand to steady himself. He wheezed and swayed for a minute, and I was sure he was going to faint. The caregiver in me wanted to comfort him, to sit him on the couch and bring him a cup of hot tea, but the part of me that had just dealt with the cops, covering up for who knew what crime, was willing to let him suffer.

Finally he raised his eyes to mine again. "Michelle's husband was murdered Saturday night."

"Michelle? Who is that?"

"The girlfriend, I'll bet." Jack had an odd little smile on his face, as if he'd figured out something ahead of the rest of the class. Maybe he had.

"Yeah, my girlfriend." Riley went back to staring at the carpet.

"You're dating a married woman?" There had been some speculation about that possibility among the poker group, but I was still a bit shocked. Not that Riley had always been staunchly moral, you understand, but he'd always had his pick of attractive, available women. Why would he go after another man's wife? And why was I more angry about *that* than the idea that maybe he'd killed someone?

"I didn't intend to. It just sort of happened."

"You mean you accidentally killed him?"

"No! Not that! I mean I didn't set out to date a married woman."

"Having an affair is pretty much a conscious choice." I heard the scorn in my tone, but I couldn't help it. Okay, I know I'm not always standing on solid moral ground myself, and I have no more right to judge than anyone else, but I was still pissed off.

"I always thought so, too." Riley sounded miserable, and not just because he had a high fever. "Then I met Michelle. I couldn't stop thinking about her. She's everything I ever dreamed of, and more! I just want to hear her voice, and touch her face, and…"

"Okay, okay!" I cut him off before it got too personal. "I get the picture."

"I doubt that. You can't understand, unless you've felt it. It's more than just falling in love… I cherish her, Rainie. I can hardly stand being away from her!"

"Sounds more like an addiction than love." Jack didn't sound impressed with Riley's fervent declarations.

"Really, this isn't some sort of sordid

affair!" Riley stared at me with those glassy, feverish eyes, willing me to believe him. "We're like... soul mates! We were meant to be together..."

He broke off abruptly, and this time I looked away. I think maybe I'd been rolling my eyes, but I hoped I'd only been doing that mentally.

"Never mind that crap," Jack interjected. "Tell us more about the dead husband."

"Oh, that." Riley sighed, as if he'd been reminded of some small but annoying detail, like the need to pick up dog crap in the yard. "He was shot Saturday night in the parking lot outside his gym. It's that new twenty-four hour place in Niles, where you let yourself in with a key card any time day or night. He'd been working out late, there was no one around. No witnesses."

"What makes you think you're a suspect?"

"Because that cop's car was in my driveway just a little while ago! I didn't think he'd come straight here to check my alibi."

"But why do they suspect you? Do they know about the affair?" That would piss me off on a whole new level. I mean, I was one of Riley's best friends, and *I* hadn't known about it.

"They don't know anything for sure, but

they checked Michelle's phone - I guess she was their first suspect."

"Sure, they always check out the spouse first." Jack nodded.

"Michelle didn't do it either!" Riley protested so vehemently he went into another coughing fit. I waited until it subsided.

"What did they find on her phone?"

"Just a text from me." He grimaced. "She usually deletes that stuff right away, you know, so Bill won't find them... wouldn't find them." Riley wiped his forehead again, as if just remembering that Bill was dead. "For some reason she missed one."

"What did the text say?"

"I'm not sure. The last thing I remember texting was about my flu, and she sent back that I should drink lots of fluids and stay in bed. Which is what I did, from about nine o'clock Saturday night until that cop pounded on my door this morning."

"So unless Michelle actually told him, the cop doesn't know about the affair."

"I know, I can't figure that out. How could he suspect? He's just a small town cop, how smart could he be?"

"A person's IQ isn't in direct correlation to the population of the city he lives in," Jack pointed out wryly. "In any case, I don't think you have anything to worry about... unless you do?"

"What? No! For God's sake *no*! I didn't kill him!" Riley nearly wailed the denial, and I blinked in surprise. How un-Riley like. He was normally so smooth, the proverbial cool cucumber. Still, I was happy to hear him deny it so fervently. It probably isn't nice to suspect your friends of murder, but then, he *had* set up an alibi months in advance.

As if reading my thoughts, Riley turned his most sincere expression on me. "Rainie, you don't really think I did it, do you?"

I stared back at him, wanting to ignore the puppy dog eyes. I have always had a soft spot for Riley, overlooking some of his worst behavior in favor of his more likable attributes. I've often made excuses for him, not just to others but to myself, because I really care about him. But haven't I always known he had just a touch of anti-social tendencies? Nothing overt, you understand. It was just as if he held an underlying belief that he was the most important person on earth and therefore some selfishness was warranted. But this wasn't just a decision to go to a football game on the day of a friend's wedding. Could Riley really justify killing Michelle's husband so he could have her to himself?

Riley looked like he might cry. "You do. You think I killed the guy."

"No, of course I don't," I lied. I mean, I didn't know for sure what I thought. Either way, he was still my friend, and it seemed he was already suffering enough. "I think you should just go home, get some rest."

"And *don't* call Michelle, whatever you do!" Jack admonished him. "Until this is over, you'd better delete her number and forget you ever met her."

"I can't do that! This could take months…"

"And if they arrest you for murder you could sit in prison for years." Jack pointed out coldly. He stepped close to Riley, all signs of amusement gone. "You listen to me! Rainie put her neck on the line for you, providing you an alibi that you might or might not deserve. Now you'd better do everything in your power to keep her out of this, or I'll see to it you don't have to worry about prison."

Riley straightened up, doing his best to overcome Jack's intimidating stance, but a couple of inches in height weren't going to do that.

"You're threatening me?"

"You're damned right I am!"

"Hey, I can look out for myself!" I protested. Jack backed off a step, but his expression didn't change. This was the cold, calculating soldier that figured the cost of one casualty against the cost of the whole battle.

"This may be one time you can't look out for yourself," he said to me. "You like this guy too much to be objective." Jack pinned Riley with that look again. "I don't have that problem."

"Okay, okay." Riley jerked his eyes away from Jack and looked back at me. "I'm sorry, Rainie. I guess I shouldn't have pulled you into this."

Huh, this was quite a day for un-Riley like behavior. He rarely found a reason to apologize.

"We're friends, Riley." Feeling bad for my suspicious thoughts, I stepped forward and hugged him. "You know I'll always be here for you."

Riley hugged me back so tightly I feared he might crush a rib. He let me go and took a step back, looking ready to cry again. "I'd better get home."

"Call me later."

I stared at the kitchen door for a long minute after he left.

"You all right?" Jack asked.

"Yeah, sure. I mean, what's to be upset about? So Riley might go to jail for the rest of his life, what's the big deal, right?"

"No need for sarcasm. Look, if you're that worried about him, why don't you look into it?"

"Look into what? You mean the murder?"

"Sure, why not?"

"Because I'm not a cop, that's why not!"

"So? Private detectives have a right to look into this sort of thing. Of course, the cops have better resources, but they don't always have the time to be really thorough."

"That Detective Williams was thorough enough to check out a single text message."

"True. On the other hand, he didn't follow up with the obvious question when he was interviewing you. If he was really on the ball he would have verified that Riley was here until the poker game broke up."

"Still, I'm sure he'll find the real killer and Riley will be off the hook."

"Or he'll focus on Riley so hard he won't bother to find the real killer."

"Come on Jack! I'm not a huge fan of the police, but I don't think the majority of them are that lazy."

"I agree. On the other hand, there are plenty of people released after serving thirty years in prison for crimes they didn't commit. Mistakes are made, whether through neglect or human error, it doesn't matter to the person whose life is ruined."

"So you think it's really possible Riley will go to jail for this, even if he isn't guilty?"

"I don't know." Jack shrugged. "Hard to say. I don't think the cops target the wrong guy on purpose; they're driven in part by statistics. In a case where there's a domestic issue, more times than not it's the spouse or the 'other person' who's responsible. If it wasn't a robbery, then who does have motive? Obviously, in this case, Riley does."

I bit my lip and glanced back at the kitchen, as if Riley was still standing there. He'd looked so freaked out, so vulnerable... I couldn't imagine him going to prison.

"Maybe you're right. I guess it wouldn't hurt to look into it a bit... but I have no idea where to start! I don't even know the dead guy's name."

"So call Riley." Jack glanced at the clock. "Look, I need to meet a guy. You start the prelims, get the guys basic info, and if you want I'll help you from there. I just need a couple of hours, okay?"

"Thanks, Jack. I appreciate it."

"I know you do," he smiled. "I haven't forgotten what I came here for, you know. Promise me you'll stay alert, and if *anything* suspicious happens - no matter how insignificant it seems - call me, okay?"

"Okay." I lied.

"And carry that pepper spray."

"I will." And that was *not* a lie. I like to be independent, not stupid.

"Don't get distracted worrying about Riley and forget about worrying about yourself."

"Hey, I'm not stupid, I won't do that."

"It isn't a matter of stupidity. It's that caregiver stuff in you; this is one time you can't be putting someone else's well-being first."

I don't think I do that; I'm pretty sure I'm just as selfish as the next person, but I didn't argue with him.

Jack gave me a look that made me think he was reading my mind, but he just shook his head. "I'll call you in a couple of hours."

"I have to be at Maggie's at eight thirty, and I'll be with her until noon anyway."

"Okay." With a wave he went out the door. As soon as he left I called Riley. He answered in a hurry.

"What? Did the cops come back?"

"No. I just wanted to know Michelle's husband's name."

"Why? Oh man, are you going to help me? Rainie, that is so cool..."

"I'm just going to look into a few things, but don't get your hopes up. I'll do what I can..."

"That's great, Rainie! Really... damn, this is such a mess."

"That's an understatement. So what's his name?"

"It's Bill... um, William, actually... William Brooks."

"Do you know a middle name? Birthdate?"

"No, but I could call Michelle..."

"No! You can't call her, Riley! Jack was right about that, you need to stop all contact with her right now."

"But Rainie..."

"Look, Riley, I'll help if I can, but only if you help yourself, too. If you can't promise me this one thing, I'm not going to waste my time."

"Damn it..." He sighed so deeply it was almost a sob.

"Give me her address. I'll go talk to her, get her husband's information, and I'll tell her about the no contact, okay?"

"Okay." Riley sighed again. "Her address is 354 East Merrifield, in Niles."

"I know the street. I'll run over there this afternoon."

"Can't you go this morning?"

"I have a client until noon."

"All right... hey, will you tell her I love her?"

"Cripes, Riley..."

"Please, Rainie... if you won't let me call her..."

"Okay, okay," I cut him off before the sobbing started. "I'll tell her. Get some sleep, I'll talk to you later."

I was going to be late if I didn't get a move on. It was a good thing Maggie had insisted I come a half hour late.

I stopped on the way out to check on George, who was just hanging out on a branch, looking his normal reptile self.

"I have to go to work."

George turned his head away to gaze at the wall, completely uninterested in how I was planning to spend my time.

"I won't be gone too late," I informed him anyway, just to be polite, and went out to my car.

# Chapter Seven

I'm ashamed to admit I probably didn't give Maggie the full attention she deserved that morning. I enjoyed going through the remaining boxes of memorabilia with her, but much of my mind was still focused on Riley's problem. I suppose I shouldn't be so hard on myself; it isn't every day you have reason to suspect one of your best friends of murder.

Maggie didn't seem to notice my distraction in any case, and she was smiling cheerfully when I left her at noon and headed over to Michelle Brook's house.

It was a neat story and a half house, the type where there might be two small bedrooms upstairs with slanted walls that followed the line of the roof. There was a tiny front yard separated from the street by a narrow, cracked sidewalk. I could see perennials just poking up from recently weeded flower beds on either side of two steps leading to the front door.

I pulled into the driveway behind a minivan with a yellow "kids on board" sign in the back window. I always wondered about those signs; did they really cause aggressive drivers to back off of their tailgating ways, or were they merely an apology from the driver for driving a minivan?

I followed a short concrete walk to the door and knocked on the aluminum screen door. I glanced around while I waited for an answer; the neighborhood was quiet, and I assumed most parents were at work while children were at school and daycare. Belatedly, I wondered if Michelle worked during the day; this might be a wasted trip. I should have asked Riley, but wouldn't he have told me that? Then again, he wasn't at his best today...

My speculation was cut off when the inner door opened on a heavy-duty chain. A tall woman with ash-blonde hair peered out at me.

"Yes?" She inquired.

"Hi, Michelle Brooks?" I tried to sound friendly and professional at the same time, like a doctor's receptionist about to inform someone that the doctor was unexpectedly delayed and their appointment would have to be rescheduled. "I'm Rainie Lovingston, a friend of Riley's."

She blinked, as if kick-starting her mental processes, and frowned slightly.

"Riley?"

"Yes. He asked me to help him out a bit with this... situation."

"I don't know what you mean."

"Look, I'm not here to cause trouble. Riley is a good friend of mine, and I already know about your... relationship. I don't plan to spread it around, but I want to help him if I can. I need some information from you if I'm going to do that."

She stared at me for a long moment. "You're his private detective friend, right?"

"An assistant," I corrected. "And this isn't going to be an official investigation. Anything you tell me is confidential and off the record." I tried for a sincere look, hoping I didn't look like a used-car salesman. "Mrs. Brooks, really, I just want to keep Riley out of prison. Please, help me do that."

She blinked again, but finally nodded and pushed the door closed far enough to work the chain loose. She reopened it and unlatched the screen door.

"Come in then."

I stepped into her small, neat living room. The room was like a miniature version of something out of "House Beautiful," so well coordinated that even I could tell it was tastefully done. The throw pillows on the sofa were covered in an eclectic mix of fabrics that I would never have thought to bring together, but which looked perfect with the dark red walls and patterned carpet. If I had tried to put this together it would have come out looking like I had picked stuff at random from other people's houses and thrown it into a junk room for later use. I just didn't get how other people could bring this stuff together and make it looked *planned*.

Oh well, I had other talents... or at least, other interests, and it was time to bring them into play.

"So what kind of information do you need?" Michelle didn't offer me a seat on her fashionable furniture or a cup of coffee, which was a shame, because I could smell some fresh brewed and it was making my mouth water. Instead she stood in front of me, keeping me effectively penned in a small area in front of the door, as if she feared that any minute I would pull out a sample case or a bible and she would need to give me the bum's rush out the door.

Michelle was tall and looked fit, a woman comfortable with her size twelve in a way that I would never be. She was wearing a t shirt and jeans, but they were clearly of the expensive, well fitted category. Her long hair was pulled back neatly into a thick ponytail held by a giant barrette. She wasn't wearing any makeup that I could see, and her eyes were a tiny bit puffy and red, as if she'd been crying not long before. I wondered if she was grieving the husband she had been cheating on, or mourning the loss of his income. I shut off that cynical line of thinking; I couldn't let my personal judgment influence me right now.

"I need to know your husband's personal info, so I can do a search on him. You know, middle name, birth date, social security number..."

"Whoa, wait a minute!" She actually held up a hand like a traffic cop. "What do you need that for? He's dead! Why would you be investigating him?"

"Because I need to find out *why* he's dead," I explained patiently. "If Riley didn't kill him, and you didn't kill him, then there must be someone else out there that had reason to want him gone."

"It might have just been a random thing." Michelle looked at the floor when she said it.

"A robbery, you mean? Was his wallet gone?"

"No." Michelle said with a sigh.

"Then that probably isn't the case."

"I know. It's just so hard to believe anyone could hate him that badly."

"Really? Pardon my frankness, Mrs. Brooks, but if you were so fond of him..."

"I know, I know!" She interrupted me. "Then why was I cheating on him? My husband wasn't a *bad* man, he was just..." She looked around the room, as if hoping the word she wanted would be printed on the walls or the ceiling. Apparently having found it somewhere, she looked back at me. "He was just busy, and a little cold... I felt as if I was just a way point for him, like an innkeeper that kept his room and cooked his meals and slept with him as part of the service. Do you see what I mean?"

I nodded, although I wasn't so sure that wasn't the case with a lot of marriages, at least from what I'd heard. My own marriage had collapsed due to completely different circumstances, but at least I had always felt Tommy's affection for me was for more than my cooking skills.

"Besides," Michelle went on, a bit self-righteously, "I *love* Riley. I mean, it isn't some cheap, tawdry affair! Riley is the man I was meant to be with all along."

"Then why didn't you leave your husband?" I asked, genuinely curious.

Michelle glared at me. "Is this information you really need?"

"It might help with motive, but not if you didn't kill him." I shrugged. "Besides, I'm just wondering. Like I said, Riley is my friend. It's only natural I would be curious why he can't be open about the great love of his life." I hoped I didn't sound snarky, because I was definitely feeling it.

"I have kids!" Michelle said it as if that should excuse her for everything from burning dinner to the Oklahoma City bombing. I just stared at her, unconvinced.

"Do you have kids?" She demanded, and I sighed inwardly. No one took my responsibilities as an iguana owner seriously. If a woman wasn't raising little people of her own, then she couldn't be admitted to that exclusive mommy club; some women acted like it had its own secret and nearly mystical code of conduct, like the Masons or the Knights Templar.

I mean, really, what's the big deal? I could easily become a mom with just one night of indiscretion, so it wasn't that difficult to join the club. Wasn't being a mother just a natural function of being a woman?

Then I remembered George lost in the trees this morning. What if that had been my imagined two year old child? Could two year olds climb like that? Would a toddler run if startled when the next random guy tackled me out of my chair?

Okay, so maybe I don't know enough about the subject to judge.

"No, I don't have kids." I belatedly answered. She was staring at me curiously, probably wondering why it took me so long to answer. I wasn't about to repeat my internal dialogue to her, so I just stood silently and waited for her.

"Well, let me tell you something about

it." Again, that self-righteous tone. "When you have children you put aside your own happiness for them. You do anything to keep them safe and happy, even if it means you can't have what you really want for yourself."

"I think I understand that," I nodded. I had heard plenty of people say they stayed together for the sake of the kids. I wasn't sure it was always the best choice, but again, who am I to know? "Do you think there's any way your husband knew about the affair?"

"How could he? He's only home two weeks out of a month, sometimes less."

"Wow. That's a lot of traveling. Is it all for business?"

"Yes. He works for a company based in Indianapolis, and he has to go to the home office every month. In between he goes to client's offices to install software."

"That must be hard on you, being alone with the kids so much." My sympathetic look was sincere this time. "It must be like being a single mom most of the time. And I'm guessing he doesn't help a whole lot when he is home."

"He doesn't. He's usually so busy being the fun dad he doesn't discipline the boys at all, just like a divorced dad... most people don't recognize that." She was looking at me with considerably less hostility.

"I can see how you would be lonely, and someone like Riley might be very appealing.

But it can't be easy, loving someone part time. I know Riley has been a mess this past year."

"I know, and I feel bad about that, but what am I supposed to do?"

I didn't know how to answer that. I'm probably the last person to be giving relationship advice, considering my own track record.

Michelle's eyes welled with tears. "It's a terrible situation, a big tragic mess, if you want the truth. I've been miserable the past year, too, and I think my kids sense that."

I wanted to say something soothing to stop her tears, but somehow Michelle had taken my claim of concern for Riley and transferred it to herself; she started pouring out her feelings as if I was her grief counselor.

"The only time I'm happy is when I'm with Riley. When I'm not with him I'm thinking about him. I want so much to introduce him to my kids, but of course I can't... I spend every spare minute I can with Riley, but then I get to feeling guilty because I'm away from the kids too much, so I push Riley away a bit. That doesn't do any good, because then I'm just missing him and I start resenting my own children for keeping me from him, and that's ridiculous, right? None of this is their fault! So in the end I feel like I'm a failure at being a mom, a wife, *and* a girlfriend."

She stopped her monologue only when her sobs overwhelmed her ability to speak. She stood there, her hands over her face, crying so hard she was bent over at the waist, almost wailing.

I reacted without thinking, the caregiver side of me shoving the cynical PI to the side. I put my arms around her and she grabbed on to me like I was a life preserver and she had been tossed overboard in rough seas. She put her head on my shoulder and sobbed into my hair, and I felt like I wanted to join her. Empathy can be a bitch.

I gently rubbed her back and let her cry, ignoring the tears and snot collecting in my hair; one thing about caregivers, when it comes to bodily fluids we're pretty much immune to gross.

After several long moments the wrenching sobs subsided to quieter gulping mewls, and finally, with a little sigh, she pulled away. She pulled tissues from her jeans pocket and blew her nose, but she didn't have enough for the job. She walked away without a word and I stood where I was, still uninvited past the doorway.

After a few minutes she came back, and stopped in the archway to the living room. Her eyes were swollen, her nose red, the hair around her forehead damp from a failed attempt to wash the signs of crying off her face.

She offered me a wan smile.

"I'm sorry, I didn't mean to break down that way."

"There's no need to be embarrassed, crying is a necessary part of grief." *Said the woman who refuses to cry in front of anyone.*

"Riley is right, you are a good person. I'm sorry I was so hostile. You want a cup of coffee?"

Now we were talking!

"I'd love some!" I enthused.

"Come on in." She gestured for me to follow her down a short hall to the kitchen. The appliances all looked new and sparkly clean, and everything was neat and orderly, except for the refrigerator. It was a cluttered mess of pictures, notes and take out menus. Predominantly featured among the chaotic paper mosaic were numerous pictures of two boys, who looked to be somewhere around the eight to thirteen year old range to my unpracticed eye. In the pictures they always seemed to be smiling, usually clowning for the camera, juvenile silliness that was at the same time pretty charming, and made me wish I could join in. Who knew kids could actually be fun?

"Do you want cream or sugar? I brew it pretty strong."

"No, black is fine, and strong is even better." I assured her.

She set a steaming mug in front of me and I nodded approval. The cup wasn't so big that I had to use two hands to pick it up, but not so small that I felt cheated. The sides were straight, so no sloshing, and the ceramic was thick enough to hold in some heat but not so thick that I would dribble when I sipped. My estimation of Michelle went up a notch: not everyone understands the importance of serving coffee in just the right mug.

"I'll try to be brief," I promised.

"It's not like I'm doing much," she shrugged sadly. "My sister took the boys today to give me a break... I don't know when I'll send them back to school... but I've just been wandering around here, dusting what I already dusted, looking at Bill's picture, crying about the whole mess."

She sat across from me with a cup of her own and looked over the rim with red, puffy eyes. "So, do you mind telling me exactly what you plan to do?"

"I wouldn't mind at all, if I knew," I answered honestly. "I've never investigated anything like this before, but I have a friend who's going to help. In the meantime, I'm just starting with the basics of any investigation: research the person's background."

"Do you really think you can figure out who killed him before the police do?"

"I don't know. The thing is, I'm worried

the police will narrow their focus on Riley, or maybe you, and they won't find the real killer."

"Why would they do that? Isn't it their job to find the truth?"

I gave her the same explanation Jack had given me, about statistics and motive.

Michelle sighed. "I guess you're right. But in spite of my misery, I didn't want Bill dead. And Riley wanted him out of my life, but he was hoping for divorce, not murder."

"I know. Riley isn't the type to kill anyone." I hoped. That disloyal voice inside my head kept wondering about Riley's self-centered tendencies. Just how far would he go to get what he thought was rightfully his? And there was still the issue of him setting up an alibi almost a year in advance...

"So if I give you this information, will you keep me in the loop if you find something?"

"Sure." *Well, mostly,* I added silently to myself. There might be some things I didn't care to share, but she didn't have to know that. "You have a right to know."

"Okay. Ask your questions."

I pulled my notebook out of my purse and prepared to write. "What's his middle name?"

"Constantine," Michelle said with a rueful smile. "Don't ask me; it's a family name."

"Should make him unique when I look

him up, at least. What's his birth date?"

We went through all the basic info, social security number, mother's maiden name, his employer, the names of close friends and acquaintances that might know something of his personal life.

"Bill didn't have a lot of friends. He worked a lot, like I said, and he wasn't the type to hang out. He wasn't much of a sports fan, didn't like bars, hated bowling and golf, thought it was all a ridiculous waste of time."

"So what did he do for relaxation?"

"He read a lot, and he'd take the boys places. You know, the park, the zoo… he had a bike, and he'd take the boys riding at the Riverwalk in nice weather, and of course, he went to the gym three or four times a week when he was home, and used hotel facilities when he traveled. He liked to stay in shape."

"He didn't have a particular friend that went to the gym with him, or another guy to ride with when he didn't take the boys?"

"Not really. Now and then he'd fire up the backyard bar b q grill and invite Greg and Tammy over from next door, but that was about it. He just never seemed to feel a need to have a lot of friends."

*Or any*, I couldn't help thinking, but I kept my editorial comments to myself.

"Do you think he might have confided in Greg if there had been something bothering him?"

"I doubt it," Michelle shook her head. "Then again, if you had asked me a week ago if there was anyone who wanted to kill my husband I would have said no way, so who knows? There must have been something going on in his life that I didn't know about."

"I think I'll at least talk to the neighbor then."

"I guess it can't hurt." Michelle sighed. "Is it crazy that part of me wants you to find out who killed him, but another part of me fears the answer? I mean, what if Bill was into something… unsavory, and that comes out in the newspapers?"

"Unsavory…?"

"Oh, I don't know what I mean exactly. It's just, if he really did do something to be murdered, not just randomly, it's probably going to be scandalous, right?" Tears were welling in Michelle's eyes again. "Not to mention that any deep investigation will probably reveal my affair with Riley. What will that do to my boys? What will my family think?"

"Maybe you should try to explain it to your kids before the papers get the information."

"Explain it how? 'Gee kids, I know Daddy is dead and all, but what the heck, I already have a new Daddy in mind…'" She broke down again, sobbing into her hands, and this time I let her cry. She was in a hell of a mess, and I certainly didn't have any sage advice to offer. I can deal with aging, failing clients and their confused, grieving families, but I had absolutely no idea how to deal with extramarital affairs and their effects on children. Maybe when she calmed down I would suggest a family counselor. I don't know that they help a lot, but a good one might at least be able to smooth the rocky road ahead of her a bit.

After a few minutes she abruptly got up and left the room, and I was left to sip my cooling coffee for a while. I looked around the immaculate room, my eyes drawn again and again to the laughing children in the pictures, their happiness recorded on shiny paper for generations to come to witness. I pulled my gaze away from their forever smiles and impatiently tapped my pen on my notebook. I didn't want to get moody about this; I needed to get the information I came for and get out of this grieving house before I started sobbing with Michelle.

She came back finally, her eyes dry and her makeup refreshed.

"Would you like some more coffee?" She asked calmly.

"Yes, please," I agreed eagerly, and held out my cup for a refill. She poured more for both of us, returned the pot to the warmer and came back to sit at the table.

"I'm sorry, where were we?"

"We were discussing Bill's friends."

"Oh yeah... I did think of one other, but Bill hasn't really spent much time with him lately. Hank Seville, an old college buddy."

"Any idea why they don't hang out anymore?"

"Not really. I thought maybe they had just drifted apart. I haven't heard Bill mention him for... oh, I don't know, a year maybe."

"And there was nothing particular going on then that might have caused a rift?"

"Nothing I remember. Bill never said they had a fight or anything, it just seemed he stopped talking about him. I can give you Hank's number; it's probably best if you ask him."

"That would be good."

Michelle got up and went to a kitchen drawer and pulled out an address book with sunflowers on the cover. She used the tabs on the side and opened to the correct page.

"Here it is: Hank Seville," she spelled the last name and read off the phone number. "He lives down in South Bend now. He's a math professor at Indiana University."

"Okay, I'll talk to him. Do you have your neighbor's number while you're at it?"

"Sure." She rattled the number off for

me. "He works nights, so he might even be home now."

"I'll check when I'm done here."

"Rainie… something else occurred to me…" Michelle was suddenly looking at me wide-eyed, her expression fearful. "You don't think Bill was involved in anything illegal, do you? I mean, something involving money or… whatever, I don't know… but, could me and the kids be in danger?"

"I doubt it," I reassured her automatically, but actually, I had no idea. "You were married to the guy; do you think he was capable of doing anything like that?"

"I don't know…" Michelle's eyes were brimming again. "To tell you the truth, these past five years or so I feel like I hardly knew him at all. He was so… distant… and gone so much… like I said, I felt like we were just a way point. Who knows what he might have been hiding?"

*Sure*, I thought. *Look how you managed to hide your affair with Riley for a whole year from him…*

Once again, I kept my snarky thoughts in my head where they could do no harm.

"I suppose, until you do know a little more about what happened to Bill, it wouldn't hurt to be more cautious. Do you know if they found Bill's keys?"

"I don't… why?"

"Just being overly cautious... I assume he had a house key on his ring?"

"Oh my god!" Michelle went pale. "Do you think whoever it was will come here..."

"I don't think so," I hurried to calm her. "But it doesn't hurt to be careful. Maybe you should have the locks changed."

"I will... right now..." Michelle started casting around the kitchen, as if she expected to find a new set of locks in a drawer somewhere that she could install herself. But no, she was just looking for a phone book.

"I just have a couple of more questions..."

"I'm sorry, I have to call someone... I can't possibly sleep here tonight if I don't get new locks!"

"I understand. Try calling Superior Safe and Lock. I know the owner, he's a really nice guy. If you explain the situation I'm sure he'll get someone out today."

"Thank you!" Michelle looked as grateful for the suggestion as she might have if I'd actually changed the locks myself. She found the number in the book and called. Once again I found myself looking around the kitchen, killing time while I waited for her to finish.

Her end of the conversation was embarrassingly tearful, but as I promised her the owner, David, was sympathetic and promised to have someone out before dark. She hung up with almost gushing words of gratitude, then turned back to me.

"He did seem nice. Thank you, Rainie. I've never had to call a locksmith before. Bill usually handled that sort of thing when he was home. I've never even had to pay the bills…"

"I'm glad he's able to help you out," I interrupted before the list of things she would have to handle for herself in the near future suddenly overwhelmed her. I was a bit surprised; with Bill gone so much, I would think she would be more prepared to handle life on her own. But maybe she had always left it for him; sort of like the mom's who tell the kids "Just wait until your dad gets home!" I hope she hadn't left all the discipline to Bill; I couldn't imagine a kid waiting two weeks to be spanked for an infraction of the rules.

"Anyway, I just have a few more things to ask…"

"Oh, of course, I'm sorry…" Michelle glanced at the clock on the stove. "I'd like to finish up before the kids get home."

"Sure, okay," I said agreeably, as if I had been the one running out of the room or picking up the phone every five minutes.

It took another cup of coffee to get everything I needed, and by the time I closed my notebook I was getting a little fidgety, feeling the urge to pee coming on. I hate using other people's bathrooms, but I hate public ones even more.

"I think this should do it, for now, so I'll just get on it and leave you to your day."

"I don't know what my days are now. It's funny how even someone you planned to divorce can leave such a big hole in your life when they're suddenly gone."

Her eyes started to well up again, and I patted her hand.

"I know, I'm sorry."

"So am I," she sighed. "And I was wrong; you would obviously make a very good mom. Look how you comforted a complete stranger..." she laughed briefly, a little snort. "You didn't even flinch with my nose running all over your shoulder, so you already have the ick factor under control."

I laughed a little at that, too. "Hair washes. So do hands..."

"And feet... maybe it's just boys, but their feet always seem to be covered in some unidentifiable goo."

That made me laugh again, thinking of my predominantly barefooted childhood. "It's not just boys."

"Any kid would be lucky to have you for a mom."

"Thanks," I squirmed, uncomfortable with the kind words and my full bladder. "I hate to ask, but can I use your bathroom? The coffee…"

"Of course." She stood, tears forgotten for the moment, and pointed down the hall. "Second door on the left."

"Thanks." I scooted off toward the promised relief.

This was obviously the boy's shared bathroom, unless Michelle was really into Spiderman. The shower curtain, bathmat and even the soap dispenser was in Spidey motif; even so, the room was almost obsessively clean. Not a speck of spit-out toothpaste in the sink, not a drop of stray soap dripped from the dispenser. I wondered if she always kept things so perfect, or if her compulsive cleaning was the result of trying to keep her mind off of her loss. Or maybe it was a case of a guilty conscience: if she had killed her husband, she might feel a need to keep moving ahead of her thoughts, or even feel compelled to make everything else in her kids' life perfect, since she had taken away their daddy…

I sighed and washed my hands. I'm not a psychologist, just a caregiver PI with a tendency to wax poetic now and then. I needed to dig into the facts and leave speculation out of the mix.

Michelle walked me to the front door, and it opened just before she could reach for the knob. A woman stepped in, looking remarkably like Michelle, albeit several years younger. Two boys came in behind her, easily recognizable from the photo gallery on the refrigerator as Michelle's sons.

She pulled them to her for a hug, one in each arm. "Hey boys, I missed you."

"You too, Mom," the older one said, but his tone was flat, as if he didn't have much emotion left in him. The younger one didn't say anything, just accepted the hug and wandered off. They were both subdued and quiet, no sign of the clowning around evident in their photographs, and it tore at my heart. How long would it take for them to get past their grief over their father and revert to the charming boys they had been before? Or would they ever?

I didn't know, and I had to put it out of my head. I couldn't fix their grief, but maybe I could get justice for their father.

Funny, people talk all the time about "getting justice," which is really just a civilized form of revenge, but somehow I didn't see how that was going to heal what was broken in those two little boys.

I sat in my car and looked over at the neighbor's house. I was strangely emotionally drained after my interview with Michelle, and wanted nothing more than to go home and curl up on my couch with a good book for a while. But I was already here; it seemed silly not to make an attempt to talk to Greg and Tammy. I reminded myself that Riley was in big trouble; if I didn't help him, who would?

I sighed and pulled out my cell phone and dialed the number Michelle had given me.

"Hello?" A bright feminine voice answered.

"Hello, my name is Rainie Lovingston. Michelle Brooks gave me your number and said it should be okay to call you." There; always start with an introduction that includes a mutual acquaintance.

"Call about what?" She still sounded friendly, but a bit more cautious.

"I'm a private investigator's assistant, and I'm looking into Bill's murder. I wondered if you and Greg would have a moment to talk to me?"

"We've already talked to the police…"

"I know," I said, knowing I would hear this from just about everyone as I followed in the footsteps of the official investigation. "But if you could just spare a few minutes, I would really appreciate it."

"When?"

"Well, I just finished talking to Michelle, so I happen to be right here… if it's inconvenient, I'll come back another time." I was trying not to be too pushy, but also, I admit, it wouldn't break my heart if she wanted to put it off. I was really not in the mood for this.

But no Tammy was in the spirit of cooperation.

"Sure, I guess that will be okay, if it's quick. I'm just fixing Greg's dinner."

"Okay, great. I'll be right there."

I hung up and took a deep breath, letting it out slowly, a relaxation technique I sometimes used, with mixed results. After several breaths I decided it wasn't going to work this time; all I was getting from it was hyperventilated.

I gave up and got out of the car.

Greg and Tammy's house looked a lot like Michelle's, except the flower beds were a bit more extensive and the lawn was a little greener, even this early in the season. Greg must be one of those guys who fertilized fall and spring, using all those chemicals that made my mom's blood boil. Perhaps literally, to hear her tell it. Someone had been out edging the grass away from the front walk; there was a neat half-inch wide furrow running along the right side of the walk. There was a pile of thin strips and clumps of grass in the middle of the walk that looked like some strange dirty green road kill animal. I stepped carefully around it, half expecting to see flies swarming it, and went up the single step to the four by four foot concrete pad that served as a front porch. Just as I lifted my hand to knock the front door swung open.

"Hi. You must be the detective, right?" The woman (Tammy, I presumed) was a shade over her ideal weight, and from the tightness of her clothes I suspected the extra pounds were a recent addition, and she was either still in denial or simply couldn't afford to shop for new clothes. She had a wooden spoon in one hand, and I hoped it was just because I'd interrupted her dinner preparations and not that she was going to smack me with it if she didn't like my looks.

"I'm Rainie Lovingston. You're Tammy?"

"Yep, that would be me." She gave me a bright smile. "Come on in, I've got stuff on the stove. Greg will be down in a minute."

"Okay." I followed her through a long, narrow living room and down a short hallway into a big kitchen. This was clearly where most of the living happened in this house. It was bigger than the living room, and a painted beam in the ceiling was testimony that they had knocked out a wall to make it so big. The appliances were clean but well worn, and the room was dominated by a scarred oak table right in the center. At the moment it was occupied by a newspaper, two coffee cups and an assortment of bowls and spoons.

"Excuse the mess, I'm about to do some baking once I finish this sauce." Tammy waved at the table. "Have a seat. Want some coffee?"

"Sure," I answered without thinking. I have a hard time saying no to coffee; so what if I didn't sleep tonight? Sleep is overrated anyway.

She poured me a cup in a thick mug and set it in front of me. "Cream and sugar if you want it." She pointed at a blue china set in the middle of the table. "So what is it you want to know about Bill? Terrible thing, right? Him being murdered and all? Poor Michelle… and those boys!" She tsked and turned to the stove to stir something that smelled strongly of garlic and onions.

"Yes, it is terrible," I agreed, thinking her tone was a bit flippant to be really sympathetic.

"Do they have any idea who might have done it?" Tammy was fishing for gossip.

"I don't believe any suspects have been named yet," I answered.

A man came in from the hallway, wearing only a low-slung pair of jeans, his hair wet and tousled as if he'd just done a quick dry with a towel. He was slim almost to the point of emaciation, and I wondered what was holding his pants up. I just hoped whatever it was, it was enough. They were hanging low enough to make it obvious he wasn't wearing underclothes, and I didn't particularly care to be flashed by his man parts.

"You the detective?"

"I'm Rainie Lovingston. I'm a private investigator's assistant."

"What, we don't rate the real thing?" He grinned, and it was one of those smiles that make me instantly want to like a person; it was amused and wry and devil-may-care all at the same time. I smiled back at him.

"I guess that depends on what you have to tell me."

"Probably not much, I'm afraid." Greg poured himself a cup of coffee and plopped down on the opposite side of the table. He pushed a stack of bowls aside so he could see me. "We didn't know Bill very well."

"Michelle said you'd talk sometimes, grill out now and then."

"Yep, and that was about it. Talked about things like the weather and what fertilizer we were using on the lawn, and why we preferred charcoal over gas grills. That's about it."

"Bill was always real friendly when we saw him," Tammy added. "We just didn't see him much."

"Yeah, he travelled a lot for his job, and when he was home he stayed inside a lot. Did the minimum on his lawn, you know; he said there wasn't much use going overboard, what with the boys playing on it and all."

"Actually, last year Brendon started

doing most of the mowing." Tammy pointed out.

"Brendon?" I asked for clarification.

"The oldest boy. Good kid. Real shame about losing his dad; hope it doesn't ruin him."

"Yeah, some boys without a father…" Tammy sighed. "Well, especially now that he's an adolescent. A boy needs a role model."

"We don't have any kids ourselves," Greg said. "But we have a couple of nieces and nephews we're pretty close to, so we know a little about it."

"Sure. It is sad," I agreed. "Did you notice any changes in Bill lately? You know, odd behavior, maybe he seemed nervous, or less friendly? Anything like that?"

"Haven't really seen him much the past couple of months, being winter and all. Just to wave to when he was out shoveling snow."

"And Brendon did most of that this year, too." Tammy sounded a bit disapproving, but I couldn't see how mowing and shoveling could be detrimental to an adolescent boy.

"So you think maybe Bill wasn't feeling well? Maybe that's why he had his son doing the outside stuff."

"I don't know about that. Did you ask Michelle?"

"No, but then she didn't mention the shoveling."

'I think it was more a matter of teaching the kid some responsibility, not to mention getting him away from computer games. You know how that can get to kids these days."

"So I've heard. What about Bill's job? Did he seem happy there?"

"Oh yeah, he loved his job," Greg nodded. "He loved the travelling."

"So he talked a lot about it?"

"Well..." Greg frowned and cocked his head to one side. "You know, now that you mention it, he really didn't. It was more an impression I got, I guess. His face would sort of light up when he'd mention he was going out of town."

"Made me feel bad for Michelle," Tammy put in. "Like he was anxious to be away from her."

"So there were problems between them?"

"Not that I ever saw," Greg shook his head. "He always treated her well from what I could see; holding her chair and stuff, even at a backyard bar b q, holding her hand when they walked over, that sort of thing."

"But at the same time... I don't know, it didn't seem real to me." Tammy argued.

"How so?" I asked.

"I don't know. It was just a little forced, you know? Like his timing was always a step behind, as if he was reminding himself to do it."

Greg laughed. "I guess she would know better than me, right? Hell, I'm just a guy, what do I know about manners?"

Tammy laughed good-naturedly. "Ain't that the truth? If Greg held my chair I'd be worried he was about to pull it away as a joke."

"Now honey, don't exaggerate. I've held your chair before."

"Yep, the night you proposed to me, and never a night since. I should have suspected something then and kept right on walking." She leaned over to give him a light kiss on top of his head.

Their easy banter had me smiling, and I felt a little guilty that I had so easily put aside my grief for the half-orphaned boys next door. I decided to return to the subject.

"Did Michelle ever say anything about Bill's behavior?"

"No, not a word," Greg assured me. "What did she have to say about it? You said you talked to her first, right?"

"Yes, just a few minutes ago, but she's understandably shaken up. I didn't want to press too hard." That was just a tiny lie, and I didn't even blush.

"I'm afraid we aren't much closer to Michelle than we were with Bill. She's a nice lady, but she's pretty wrapped up with her boys when Bill is away. We don't see her much."

"I understand. Well, I appreciate you taking the time to talk to me." I fished a business card out of my purse. "If you think of anything else, will you please call me? Any little thing might help."

"Sure, if we think of anything." Greg pinched my card between two fingers and held it out to Tammy, who plucked it away from him and stuck it under one of a couple of dozen

"I hope they figure out who did it." Tammy turned from her cooking to look at me. "You know, on TV they always look at the wife first in this kind of case."

"Yes, well, lucky for Michelle this isn't TV." I smiled to keep my comment from sounding snotty.

"I noticed someone picked the boys up this morning," Tammy said almost too casually. "I was a little worried that maybe it was Child Protective Services."

"Why would you think that?" I tried to keep the scowl off my face at her obvious attempt to glean some ugly morsel about Michelle to share on the gossip circuit.

"Well, if they suspected Michelle of murder, it would only make sense they would take the boys for their own protection, right?"

"So far as I know they don't do any such

thing unless a person is convicted. Innocent until proven guilty, right?" I put a little steel in my voice, but then backed off to a more pleasant tone. It wouldn't do to alienate one of my few sources of information, even if it didn't seem to be getting me anywhere. "I think it's more likely a family member took the boys for a while, to give Michelle some time to herself. She really is pretty broken up about this."

"Oh, I didn't think of that." Tammy looked disappointed at having her theory shot down; I was liking her less and less, and wondered what Greg saw in her. He seemed so open and genuinely concerned in contrast to his wife.

"I wish we could have been more help," Greg jumped back in to the conversation, after flashing a brief look of…what…disgust maybe… at his wife's back.

"Do you think they're looking at her for this?" Unlike his wife, Greg sounded genuinely concerned by the possibility. "That would be a hell of a thing for those boys. A hell of a thing!"

"Yes it would, but I don't think she's a suspect. I haven't heard anything, anyway," I lied again. I didn't want Michelle to become the subject of yet more neighborhood gossip.

"Glad to hear that." Greg stood to walk me out; Tammy had lost interest in me, sensing that I wasn't going to reciprocate by sharing any information with her. Oh well, there was another lost opportunity to make a new friend. Not.

## Chapter Eight

**I** considered my next move as I drove home. I wasn't really sure how to pursue this investigation. I know how to locate missing persons and dig all the dirt up from someone's past, but how to go about figuring out who murdered a man I didn't know?

Besides, this was another case where I was on my own, without the considerable resources of B&E Security to back me up. I couldn't access their data bases and search services without talking to Harry Baker, and no way was I going to do that this time. In the back of my mind there was still that nagging little thought that just maybe Riley was guilty; if I found evidence to prove that...

Well, I didn't care to think what I would do about it, but I was pretty sure I didn't want B&E's official involvement.

Jack had promised to help, and he did seem to have a lot of private sources of information, but I didn't want to just sit around and wait for him; certainly I could do some more basic ground work on my own. I would call when I got home and set up a time to talk to Bill's friend, Hank, but I didn't particularly want to talk to him today. The weather was gorgeous, the warm wind blowing through my open car window begging to be breathed in and promising great fun if I would only go out and play in it.

But Riley was in trouble; I couldn't just blow it all off.

I had all of Bill's personal information, including the company he worked for; could he have pissed off a coworker bad enough to get himself killed? Maybe someone passed over for promotion because of him, or even fired... that sort of thing happened all the time, but would someone actually kill because of it?

I suppose that depended on how good the job and/or promotion was. It was at least worth looking into. I decided an internet search on his company was as good a place as any to start.

I got home and went straight to George's cage.

"How're you feeling?" I asked him. He blinked at me, then moved up his branch, waiting to be let out, which said to me he was feeling just fine.

"Okay, come on out," I said as I opened the door. "I'll get you some goodies."

He made himself comfortable under his

heat lamp while I went to fill his bowl with fresh fruit and veggies. He dove right in when I put it in front of him; a non-iguana owner would probably shake their head over my relief at this proof of his continued good health.

My answering machine was flashing, so I hit play and listened while I moved around the living room, straightening what little needed to be straightened. There were three messages, two of which were hang ups. The third was a high pitched squeal that I thought might be a fax machine. I so rarely got calls on the home phone I was thinking I really should have it disconnected and save the expense. My mother would just have to get used to calling my cell. As for all those business cards I had passed out with the home number on it, I was pretty sure the phone company would give out my cell number for a few months. I could get new cards made up, they didn't cost much, and start passing them around town...

My mind was wandering again; I needed to sit down and look up Bill's company, but I felt restless and out of sorts. If only I could go out and smoke a cigarette, that always helped me focus...

"Stop that." I ordered myself curtly. Okay, then maybe I could go pick up a bag of chips... or some chocolate. Yeah...

"Oh no, you don't!" I firmly squashed

that copout. I would rather smoke than be fat again. "I'm going for a walk around the block," I told George. "Be good."

The walk helped a little, but I couldn't get my head completely away from the need for a smoke. I had read that the urges only lasted a few seconds, but what they hadn't mentioned was that the urge kept coming back every two minutes. How long did it take for the withdrawal symptoms to pass? I felt shaky and had a headache, and I was really beginning to question the wisdom of quitting. What was wrong with doing something that made me feel so good?

But then I remembered the shortness of breath; it didn't really make me feel that good. Besides, did I want to let something have so much control over me?

I went in to take a shower. You can't smoke in a shower; maybe I could just stay in there for three days until the cravings were gone.

After my shower I settled at my desk with a spoonful of peanut butter and a glass of water and got on line. I did a Google search for William's employer, a company called OD&D, Inc., short for "Office Data and Documenting Incorporated."

Their website was a sleek, professional

looking affair that made me wish I needed their considerable services; it screamed technical prowess that inspired confidence in the company's ability to deliver as promised.

    I don't know a lot about running an office, but it seemed that OD&D could do it all, from scanning and filing every document a company needed into a searchable database, to controlling invoices, shipping and receiving, payroll, human resources and even how much toilet paper was used in the employee restrooms. And all of this, if I was reading it correctly, with one deluxe application of their software, which ultimately would lead to a "paperless office."

    According to Michelle, Bill's job had been to install the software on a company's server and train them in its basic use. I assumed, since Bill regularly traveled two weeks out of every month, that the company must sell a lot of software packages.

    Personally, while the environmentally conscious side of me liked the idea of an office being "paperless," the idea of having all my information stored on a server, or worse, in a "cloud," horrified me. I thought of Mason, also a software guy, and how easily he had hacked into a number of "secure" websites on my behalf. He was able to do it after admittedly being out of the game for a while; what about those geeky guys whose whole lives were spent in front of a bank of computers, completely devoted to honing their hacking skills. They could probably crack OD&D's software in seconds. The whole system seemed way too vulnerable to me.

Of course, I'd only recently given into the pressure of a few friends to go on Facebook. My mother was sure the whole thing was a plot by the government to gather information on American citizens through complicated algorithms and search engines. I must admit, seeing how it profiles me and puts "targeted ads" on my page, it does seem they are gathering more information than I'd like. On the other hand, I don't do much more than make inane comments on pictures of my friends' children, and I'm pretty sure that if I don't try to hatch a plot to overthrow the government and post it, there won't be any black ops troops kicking my door down.

My tummy was rumbling, and I remembered that I never had gotten around to eating anything but a couple tablespoons of peanut butter. I shut off my computer and went to the kitchen to scrounge up some food.

Jack called me at ten o'clock, just as I was thinking about going to bed.

"Hey." I answered.

"Sorry I couldn't get back to you today," he said without offering me details. "What did you find out about our dead guy?"

"Not much," I admitted. "I spoke to Bill and Michelle's neighbors, but they didn't know much. I do have a number for a friend of Bill's, but I haven't set anything up with him yet."

"You're right, that isn't much. Having some trouble focusing?"

"What?" I was startled that Jack had figured me out so easily, but he just laughed.

"I used to smoke. I remember how hard it was to quit."

"*You* smoked?" I was astonished. I couldn't imagine him ever doing anything to gum up the works of that fabulous machine of a body he had.

"Sure, I started when I was twelve; it was great for my tough guy image. Even kept it up through basic training, but I couldn't do Special Ops with compromised lungs. Anyway, it'll get better, I promise."

"All I want to do is eat."

"So, go ahead. So what if you gain a couple pounds? You'll feel so much better not smoking you'll end up burning it off again."

"Right." Not going to happen. "I did check out his company's website. It looks like a pretty big deal, based in Indianapolis. Bill was a software tech, traveled two weeks out of the month."

"Huh, that's a lot for a family man."

"I thought so, but then again, might be

better than seeing the same face over the breakfast table every single morning for fifty years."

"So young to be so cynical," Jack laughed. "So that's our place to start: Indianapolis, to talk to his boss and his coworkers, see who hated him enough to kill him. When do you want to go?"

"Oh, um... " I was stalling, because I couldn't quite imagine being in a car with Jack for three straight hours one way, yet alone another three to get home. What would we talk about? I had enough trouble keeping up a conversation with him over lunch without saying something completely stupid.

"How about tomorrow?" He suggested.

"I can't... I'm with Thelma."

"Bring her along."

"No, Jack. I've told you before, I won't involve her in my PI work."

"Hey, this isn't going to be any big deal, we're just going to talk to a few people."

"That's what you *always* say, and you know it's *never* that simple."

"Actually, it usually is. I think maybe you're a good luck charm or something."

"Good luck? Are you kidding me? I keep getting shot at or tackled by hairy men with bad breath!"

"Exactly!" Jack laughed. "Interviews are always a lot more fun with you around. Come on, Thelma would love it."

"Look, in spite of the fact that Thelma is my best friend, she still pays me to be her caregiver, so even if I wasn't going to keep her away from danger as a friend, my caregiver duties absolutely obligates me to do that."

"You have also told me that a caregiver does everything she can to enhance the client's quality of life. Do you really think keeping Thelma safe and at home makes her happy? Hell no! That lady wants to go out and have some fun!"

"She can go golf with Gary for fun. Besides, there wouldn't be room in your truck for all three of us, and I can't imagine you want to ride down there in my Escort."

"You've got that right! Not a problem, though. I can borrow Eddie's Charger, he can use my truck."

Damn, he had an answer to all my objections. I considered it; what was the big deal? He was right, Thelma loved road trips. Besides, she could help fill in the conversational gaps.

"All right, Jack, I'll ask her... "

"Great! Did you get a phone number for his employer? I'll call in the morning and set up an appointment with his boss."

I sighed. I guess there was no point in saying I would call him when I got Thelma's answer; I knew as well as he did that she wouldn't say no. I gave him the information.

"I'll pick you up at Thelma's at eight thirty."

"Okay." But I was speaking to dead air; he had already disconnected.

As predicted, Thelma was more than up for a road trip. She jumped into the back of Eddie's sleek black Charger like a teenager heading out to Coney Island for the day. I slid into the front, loving the almost sensuous feel of the butter soft leather. It was chilly outside, but Jack had activated the heaters in the seats, and it was like sliding into a warm embrace...

"Nice car," I understated.

"Yeah," Jack ran a hand over the curvy dashboard like it was his lover's thigh. "I'm thinking I might trade in my truck for one of these."

"What? But that's a great truck!" Thelma protested, sticking her head between the bucket seats. "It suits you." She nudged him with her elbow. "I like the fact that you don't feel a need to drive an oversized truck for compensation..."

"Thelma!" I glared at her, appalled, but her and Jack both laughed.

"You can't be leaning up here like that," I told her, anxious to steer the subject in another direction. "You need to put your seatbelt on."

"Oh, come on..."

"Thelma..."

"Right, right..." she sat back and fastened her seatbelt, muttering something that sounded suspiciously like "stick-in-the-mud old fuddy-duddy."

"Did you get an appointment with Bill's boss?"

"He'll give us a few minutes before lunch if we can get there by eleven forty-five."

"We should make that easy."

"I'm sure we will."

No one said much as Jack maneuvered through Buchanan, the car seeming to crawl at the posted twenty-five mile an hour speed limit. It was a relief to hit the bypass, where Jack quickly got the big car up to seventy miles an hour and settled in for the long cruise. He had his left hand draped over the top of the wheel, his right hand resting on his thigh. Weird how a guy like Jack can even make driving look sexy.

He clicked on his MP3 player, which was attached to a cord in one of many outlets on the car's stereo. It looked as though it was equipped to handle anything from an iPod to a ham radio hook up to a NASA satellite feed.

It wasn't long until Thelma was leaning between the seats again. I turned to say something, but she grinned and pointed at the belt around her waist; she had loosened the belt to its farthest extension. "Hey, I'm wearing it!" She grinned and I just shook my head.

"What's that you're listening to?" She asked Jack. "Is that the blues? I don't have the blues, do you? How about some rock & roll?"

Jack held the MP3 player out to her.

"Knock yourself out."

"Cool, let's see what you've got..." she started paging through the list. "Hmm... Cake... Datarock... Devo? Seriously, Jack?"

He grinned and shrugged. "I have eclectic taste."

"You might be interpreting the word 'taste' a little loosely there... wait, what's this, Duke Tomato? Now there's some party music." I laughed, imagining Thelma in a bar partying with Duke Tomato. He was pretty big in Chicago and the surrounding area, but I didn't know if his albums had ever made it big nationally. The guy really knew how to put on a show, though.

She selected a song, and I cringed when "I Want to Tie You Up" started.

"Crank it up, Jack! Let's see what kind of speakers this baby has..."

Grinning, he obliged, and for a while no conversation was possible. Thelma was belting out the lyrics from the back seat, bopping her head and snapping her fingers and just having a grand old time.

Did I say old? Probably not an

appropriate word to use with Thelma.

I was cringing and looking out the window, embarrassed to be listening to the fun but dirty lyrics with Jack sitting right next to me. "I want to tie you up! In a bathtub full of may-o-naise!" Thelma sang. I slumped a little in my seat and willed the car to move faster. It was going to be a long day.

Fortunately, Thelma settled down a bit by the time we got past Plymouth. The music was turned down and we fell into normal conversation, as adults do on long car trips. Well, normal considering the people involved. The subjects included everything from the best designed gun for arthritic hands to whether religious sacrifices were moral if they were part of your belief system, to the best method for getting blood out of a leather jacket. (The answer to that, if you for whatever reason don't want to take your bloody clothing to a professional cleaner, is to use hydrogen peroxide. Just one of many pieces of knowledge in my head that I hope I never need.)

We passed by cornfields punctuated here and there by tiny towns that barely rated the ink needed to print them on a map, and the giant wind farm that detractors say kill lots of birds, although I watched carefully as we passed and didn't see a single sparrow sucked in to the swooping blades, so who knows? Along the way we saw that other sure harbinger of spring: orange barrels. Hundreds... no, thousands of them. They are in the process of building a major limited access highway from South Bend to Indianapolis, and while I know eventually it will make the trip quicker, for a few years it's just slowing things down. Not to mention, the new bypass will leave another string of small towns behind it to die without through traffic to pump some money into them. Sadly for the small towns, the politicians were only interested in the big cities with a higher concentration of votes; they cared little if the handful of voters in Lapaz, Indiana lost their livelihoods.

 I must have been brooding about the whole thing, because Jack suddenly nudged me.

 "Hey, what are you so deep in thought about?"

 "What? Oh... I was just thinking about the new bypass, and how it's going to leave so many little towns high and dry."

 "Yeah, that bugs me, too."

 "It does?" I couldn't hide my surprise.

 "I have an affinity for small towns. how could you not know that?" he flashed me a look I couldn't interpret. "B&E's main office is in Chicago, and you know I go there and Detroit for most of my work, yet I choose to live in Niles and hang out in Buchanan. If I didn't like small towns, it would be a hell of a lot easier for me to get an apartment in Chicago."

"Huh. Funny, I never thought about it." And I did think it was odd that I had never considered it. Jack seemed to be such a huge presence in my life, yet I always thought of him as so secretive and mysterious. Now I wondered: was he really? Or was I so blinded by my insecurity when I was around him that I just didn't read the obvious clues that were there?

"What?" He asked, and I realized I was staring at him while I worked all that out in my head.

I blushed. "Nothing. You know how my mind wanders."

"I do," he agreed, and somehow that sounded like an accusation. And maybe it was; maybe Jack paid more attention to my life than I paid to his. Huh.

I decided I would rather think about that later, in private. I turned up the tunes and let the subject drop.

## Chapter Nine

We reached Indianapolis and Jack engaged the GPS embedded in the car's dashboard. It led us unerringly to OD&D Inc.'s corporate offices. They were located in a long, low building that, according to the signs at the parking lot entrance, also housed a computer sales and service store, an upscale workout center, a tax preparation office and a Subway restaurant.

The building looked well-maintained, built of stone blocks painted a brilliant white, with neat but minimal landscaping in a strip of earth that ran across the front. The parking lot was like any lot you would expect to find in front of a strip mall, the spaces clearly marked with yellow lines that looked as fresh as the paint on the building.

"Okay, let's do this," Jack said.

"This will be fun!" Thelma already had her seatbelt unfastened and was scooting toward the door.

"Wait a minute!" I protested. "I thought you would wait out here."

"What? Why?" Thelma frowned, one hand on the door handle.

"Because, you aren't a private investigator. You're just along for the ride."

"You aren't a PI either!" Thelma pointed out.

"No, but I at least work for a PI firm."

"I think I've managed to help you out a time or two. I should get to come in."

"Actually, Thelma, Rainie might be right," Jack spoke up. "Not because you wouldn't be good at this, because I'm sure you would be, but because three people might seem like overkill for a simple interview. We just want information; we aren't planning to storm the place."

"Hmph." Thelma sat back and crossed her arms. "I wasn't planning on doing anything of the sort."

"I'm sure you weren't *planning* to," Jack grinned. "But sometimes your enthusiasm carries you away."

"Only if the situation warrants it!"

"I promise, Thelma, if anyone needs to be intimidated, I'll come out and get you, okay?"

"You are so damned funny!" Thelma glared at Jack, but I could see a tiny smile threatening to quirk up the edge of her mouth. "Fine, I'll wait here, but if anything good starts to happen, you come get me!"

"We will, I promise!" Relieved, I hurried to get out of the car before she could change her mind.

Jack flashed his B&E I.D. at the receptionist, and her eyes widened a bit. She was easily in her sixties, with that red-orange hair that only modern chemicals can produce, but the garishness of her hairdo was offset by a neat, conservative pant suit and understated makeup.

"A private investigator? What do you want with us?"

"Not all of you," Jack winked at her. "We're have an appointment with Sean Whitman regarding a confidential matter."

"Ohh... is this about Bill Brooks? Such a shame, he was such a nice guy!"

"Did you know him well, Beth?" I asked sympathetically, using her name from the name plate on her desk to enforce that personal connection that makes people so much more inclined to share information. Of course, she might just be filling in for Beth, and in that case, the ploy would backfire.

"Well, not too well," Beth answered me, and I hid a tiny smile of relief. "But of course we'd talk whenever he came in for the monthly meetings, and he would bring me candy on holidays. Like I said, a nice guy. So do you think you'll figure out who... you know... killed him?"

"We certainly hope so, Beth," Jack told her sincerely. "Tell me, did everyone here think he was such a nice guy? I mean, I'm sure he only brought candy for his favorites."

Beth blushed a bit. "Well, most of the ladies here liked him really well, if you want the truth. There aren't many of us, but he was always respectful and kind, much nicer than the other men here, and he never made those little rude remarks..." She turned her gaze to me. "You know the type I mean?"

"Sure, just enough to be insulting without crossing the line to sexual harassment."

"Exactly!" Beth flashed a brief glare at Jack, as if he'd just put his hand on her butt, and looked back to me. "Some men simply have no idea how boorish they come across. I swear, most of them think we *like* that sort of trash talk!"

"Clueless," I agreed, keeping our rapport going. 'So how did Bill get along with the men?"

"Oh, everyone liked Bill. He was very personable."

Before I could ask another question a door behind the receptionist opened and a tall, fleshy man appeared in the doorway.

"Beth, are these people here to see me?"

"Oh, yes, Mr. Whitman, I was just about

to buzz you..."

"No need." He crossed the small area in lumbering strides and stuck out his hand to Jack. "Sean Whitman, Service Manager." I could have figured that out all by myself. Mr. Whitman was wearing a photo ID with the OD&D logo on it, clipped to his shirt pocket.

"Jack Jones, and my associate, Rainie Lovingston." Jack shook the guy's hand, and I put my hand out. Whitman's hand was slightly moist, and his grip was weak, but I wasn't sure if that was in deference to me being a woman; some men seemed to think it was still inappropriate to shake hands with a woman, and "held back," as if in fear our fragile hands would crack under the manly pressure. I hushed that sarcastic little voice; I hated it when she made snap judgments like that.

"Come on back to my office where we can talk in private." He flashed a look at Beth, probably angry that she might have been revealing too much about a former employee and opening the company up for a slander lawsuit. Sadly, in our litigious society, that was a definite possibility. That would make a PI's job a lot harder, if only for the fact that so many employees, not in the line of fire for such a lawsuit, love to gossip. "Beth, where's your ID? You know you aren't to be clocked in without it. I should write you up." His tone was petulant; a petty tyrant meting out petty punishment.

"Sorry," Beth hurriedly reached into a desk drawer and pulled out a plastic ID card. "I just forgot."

Whitman let her go with another glare.

We followed Whitman through the door into a large carpeted room filled with maybe ten round tables and chairs. The walls were decorated with motivational posters and write on/wipe off boards. There was a raised dais at one end with a lectern and a microphone. I thought the microphone was a bit of an overkill; even with a cold I was pretty sure I could make myself heard at the back of this room. In any case, I engaged my amazing detective skills and determined that this was the room in which OD&D Inc. held its monthly meetings.

I glanced at the white boards, which still had notes from the last meeting: "sales forecasts" "win-win" and "out of the box" among them. I couldn't help a little grimace of distaste, and once again I thanked myself for being smart enough to stay out of the corporate world. I have a tendency to roll my eyes when I hear all those cutesy buzz words and coined phrases, and I fear if I spent my days listening to them I would soon enough end up as googly-eyed as a broken doll.

Whitman led us along the edge of the room to another door with a "Sean Whitman,

Software Service Manager" stenciled on it in gold letters. It was a decent sized office, the carpet a little thicker than in the meeting room. There were lots of framed certificates on the walls, a big desk, two filing cabinets and two visitor's chairs, which Whitman waved us to on his way to his much more comfortable looking desk chair.

"Have a seat." He settled behind his desk, which was somewhat cluttered with paperwork, a small stack of books that appeared to be instruction manuals, several photos that I guessed were his wife and kids, and another nameplate reading "Sean Whitman, Software Service Manager," just in case his visitors had forgotten who he was since they took the three steps past the door.

Jack and I had barely put our butts in the chairs before Whitman leaned forward and said, "So, you're here about Bill. I still don't understand what you think you can do that the police can't, but I'm willing to help if I can. Damned shame what happened to him. One of our top men, a real asset to the company."

I noticed he only mentioned Bill's value to the company; there was nothing personal in it. Jack must have noticed, as well.

"How well did you know Mr. Brooks, on a personal level?" Jack asked.

"Oh, well, we worked together, had lunch a few times, but we didn't really hang out. Not proper between corporate levels, you understand? If I get too buddy-buddy with a subordinate there are all kinds of ways that can turn on me, accusations of favoritism and the like."

"Okay, but on a professional basis you got along?"

"Sure. Bill was a real team player, always on top of things, ready to take on a new challenge."

"What exactly was Mr. Brook's job?" I asked.

"Oh, Bill was one of our top software support specialists. I swear he could have taught an orangutan how to operate our software... not that I'm comparing our customers to monkeys, you understand, but some of them are better at new technology than others."

"So his extensive travel was for the purpose of training new customers on the use of your product?"

"Extensive travel?" Whitman blinked. "Bill did his work over the phone or online. Our installers travel a lot, but Bill was promoted past that a few years ago. The only traveling he does is to come here once a month for the company meeting."

Hmm, that was interesting. Then just where did he go two weeks out of the month?

"What if a customer couldn't

understand what Bill was telling them over the phone? Wouldn't that require a personal visit?"

"Not at all. We have the technology to take over a customer's computer and actually guide their mouse; Bill could demonstrate pretty much anything remotely. What makes you think he traveled a lot?"

"Just an impression we got, obviously we heard wrong," Jack waved the question off as unimportant. "Can you tell us about his relationships with other coworkers? Were there any hard feelings over a missed promotion or unequal pay, anything of that sort?"

"Absolutely not. We have a tight corporate structure here, promotions and pay raises are determined on a points system. There's simply no reason for any cutthroat tactics at OD&D."

"What about personal relationships?" I asked. "Maybe an office romance gone sour..."

"No way. Bill was only here one day out of the month for the corporate meeting. He barely knew anyone here well enough to have lunch with, let alone to sleep with. I'm sorry, but I really think you're barking up the wrong tree here. Whoever shot Bill, I seriously doubt if there was any connection to OD&D."

"Fair enough," Jack nodded. "In that case, would you care to speculate on anything in his personal life that might have gotten him killed?"

"No, sorry. I told you, I only had a professional relationship with him. I knew very little about his personal life, and that's how corporate prefers it."

"When was the last time you saw Mr. Brooks?"

Whitman looked at me, the hint of a frown forming. "At the last corporate meeting, of course. That would have been... " he consulted a calendar on his expansive desk. "Nine days ago, on the fourth."

"Did you notice anything different about him? Was he nervous, or seem upset?"

"Not at all. He was pretty happy, as a matter of fact. Something about his kid getting accepted into some exclusive preschool."

"Preschool?" I thought about his boys; I wasn't an expert on judging the age of kids, but I was fairly certain both his sons were well past the preschool age.

"Yes, or something to that effect. Honestly, he could have said the kid was going to college for all I really remember. I'm afraid I was pretty distracted, getting ready for the meeting. We had the CEO coming in for it, and I had a major presentation to give."

After that, there wasn't much more information forthcoming, in spite of questions from both Jack and me. Either Sean Whitman really hadn't known much about William Brooks, or he was staunchly toeing the company line, refusing to give out anything but the most basic of facts.

I accepted another damp, limp handshake from him, and surreptitiously wiped my hand on my skirt on the way out.

As soon as we were outside I asked the question I knew had to be in Jack's mind, as well. "So, where do you suppose Bill goes two weeks out of every month?"

"I suspect if I knew that, I would probably also know who killed him." Jack grinned. "I think we're on to something here."

I wasn't terribly surprised to find that Thelma was not waiting in the car when we approached it. Nonetheless, I was a bit exasperated.

"Now where did she go?" I looked at Jack, who was smiling that amused little smile he so often got when he was dealing with Thelma. I swear the guy has some sort of weird crush on her.

"I'm sure she's close by." He glanced around the parking lot, as if expecting to find her crouching behind another car, waiting to jump out and yell "gotcha!"

"We're probably lucky she didn't take off with the car. I knew leaving her the keys was a bad idea."

"Hey, I had to let her roll the windows

down if she got too warm."

"She could have just as easily opened the door." I took a look around myself, but no Thelma. The only activity seemed to be centered at the sub shop, which looked pretty crowded. Well, it was lunchtime.

"Maybe she got hungry." I pointed at the restaurant.

"Probably," Jack nodded and headed toward the shop. I hurried to catch up with him.

Jack pulled the door, then stepped back and waited while three men carrying wrapped sandwiches exited. They were all wearing the now familiar OD&D photo ID tags clipped prominently on their shirts.

We stepped inside to what might have been mistaken for a corporate meeting if not for the nationally recognized sub shop colors and logos on the walls. Just about every person in the restaurant was wearing a corporate ID tag... except, of course, for Thelma, who was holding court at one of a handful of bright green tables with three young men, all dressed in business clothes, all wearing the OD&D IDs. They were all gazing at Thelma, who said something that made them burst out laughing.

I started toward the group, but Jack stopped me with a light touch on my arm. "Let's grab a sandwich and another table, give her a chance to do her thing."

"Her thing?" I tried to keep my voice as low as his, but I was a bit incredulous. "Jack, you know how Thelma's things usually go... "

"Hey, she's a smart lady, and those guys are obviously smitten with her. Come on, I'm hungry anyway."

I sighed and followed Jack to the counter. We ordered subs (mine with extra sweet onion sauce. I don't know what they put in that stuff, but it's like the crack cocaine of fast food, I always want more!) Jack led us to a table close enough to Thelma for us to overhear the conversation.

Thelma was wearing a be-jeweled headband today, holding back her shoulder length hair in a style that looked surprisingly girlish considering it had far more gray than the original brunette in it. She was leaning toward the young men, her eyes bright and warm. For their part, they seemed to be hanging on every word she said, almost eager to please.

"Good grief!" I whispered to Jack. "Thelma has groupies!"

He grinned. "No big surprise. Look how she's working them. They love her!"

I watched them talking to her and it occurred to me why they were so anxious to answer her questions. She wasn't just pretending to be interested in what they had to say, she was clearly enjoying their company and conversation, hanging on their every word just as they were hers. She had them eating right out of her hand.

One of the guys, with a thick head of almost-too-long hair whose name tag read "Jerry H." was speaking: "...good enough guy, pretty quick with a joke."

"Good enough you say," Thelma prompted him. "But was he the type to be a bit cutthroat? You know, the kind of guy who undermines a coworker to get a promotion?"

"Nah, our company doesn't work that way." This from a thin young man whose back was to me. "Promotions are handled on a strict points basis, at least until you get to upper management, and frankly, those guys are hardly ever chosen from among us software geeks."

"Yeah, they use headhunters to find their management. Bill was pretty much at the top of where he was going, promotion-wise."

"Always raises to get, though," Jerry was quick to point out. "It's not like we can't make more money, if we get the right points, but the home office gig is about the best we can expect."

"Yeah, I'd like to get to that, myself," the thin man said. "I mean, you still have to put in the hours, but it sure would be nice not to have to commute, and to work in your pajamas all day if you want."

"The problem is, if you work at home people tend to think you don't work at all." Jerry objected. "Always asking you for favors, thinking you have nothing but time. I worked from home for my last job and couldn't wait to go back to a regular office."

"Okay," Thelma nodded and made a note in a little 3x4 inch notebook on the table in front of her, the little spiral things you could buy three for a dollar in any drugstore. She flipped back a page as if consulting her notes, looking rather professional about it, I must admit, and asked a new question. "Can you think of any other reason someone at OD&D might be angry enough with Bill to shoot him?" She lowered her voice just a bit, a subtle promise to keep whatever they said to herself. "How about lady friends?"

"Oh, like an affair?" This was the first time I'd hear the third guy speak. He was a slightly overweight specimen with thick glasses, which he pushed up his nose when he leaned forward to answer Thelma. "You think he cheated on his wife and she killed him?"

"Oh, I don't speculate on that sort of thing," Thelma shook her head. "I have to gather a lot more information before I can draw any type of conclusions."

"I saw a picture of his wife once," Jerry grinned a bit lasciviously. "She was a good looking woman; he'd be a fool to cheat on her."

"Yeah, well some guys don't know when they've got it good," the thin guy said. "And the truth is, Bill always seemed a little too friendly with the women."

"Too friendly?" Thelma prompted. "How so?"

"He flirted with all of them," the thin guy said, and I detected a bit of a tone there... maybe bitterness? "They all loved him, hung on every damn word he said, always batting their eyelashes at him and all that crap."

"Hey, it wasn't that bad," Jerry laughed. "But I will agree the ladies loved him. He was the kind of guy who remembered stuff, you know? Like if someone was getting married or a sister was having a baby, he'd remember to ask about it, maybe bring some little gift or whatever. Women love that kind of thing, makes it seem like a guy is actually paying attention."

"Yeah?" The heavy guy grinned at Jerry. "If you know so much about women, why aren't you married?"

"Probably because he knows so much about women," Thelma suggested, and all three men laughed.

She waited for the laughter to subside. "Was there any one woman in particular he seemed to be interested in?"

"I don't think so," Jerry shrugged and looked at the others for confirmation.

"Not that I ever saw," the heavy man said. "Seemed to me he was interested in them all, young old, fat, skinny, pretty... he even got friendly with that lady down in shipping, the one with the big thingy on her neck?"

"Cindy," the thin guy supplied. "And that's a birthmark, so it isn't nice to point it out; it's not like she can help it."

"Yeah, well she could help not wearing clothes two sizes too small that show off every roll in her chubby butt."

"Who are *you* to call someone chubby?"

"Hey, I know I need to lose a few pounds, but I at least I buy clothes that fit!"

"Did any of the women seem more interested in his attention?" Thelma drew their attention back to her and away from their little squabble. "Any of them seem infatuated beyond a little flirting?"

"Not that I ever noticed," the thin guy answered, and the other two shook their heads.

"Bill always wore his wedding ring," Jerry mentioned. "I mean, it was a thick band, couldn't miss it; I don't think he ever led any of the ladies on."

"Did any of you ever meet his wife?" Thelma asked. "I know she probably didn't come down here very often, living so far away, but maybe a Christmas party or something like that?"

"Our Christmas parties are held like

company meetings, no spouses invited," the heavy guy said. "But why do you say she lives so far? Terre Haute isn't that long a drive."

"Terre Haute?" Thelma asked curiously. That was a city not far from Indianapolis.

"Yeah, isn't that where he lived?" The heavy guy looked at Jerry.

"I don't know," he shrugged. "I know he didn't live in the city, but I never really asked exactly where he did live."

"I don't know either." The thin guy shook his head.

"Well, I could be wrong." The heavy guy frowned. "It's not like I was ever at his house. Could be I just assumed he lived there. He'd talk about his commute now and then, and a lot of OD&D guys live in Terre Haute."

"Yeah, the cost of living is a lot lower and the commute isn't too bad."

"Especially when you only have to come to the office once a month."

"Hey guys, it's getting late." Jerry glanced at his phone. "I'm really sorry, Thelma, but we have to get back. We lose points if we're late."

"Sure boys, I understand," she grinned at them. "You've been very helpful, I really appreciate it."

"I've never met a real PI before," the thin man smiled eagerly. "This has been pretty cool."

They all stood and gathered their empty sandwich wrappers.

"You certainly aren't how I pictured a private detective," the heavy man told her. "But you seem to be pretty good at it. I hope you figure out what happened to Bill."

"Yeah, he deserves justice." Jerry said.

"Unless he was messing around on his wife," the thin man smiled. "Then maybe he got what he had coming."

"Karma's a bitch." Thelma nodded seriously, and all three men laughed.

"You're okay, Thelma," Jerry told her. He handed her a business card. "That has my cell on it. If there's anything else you think I can help with, give me a call."

"Oh yeah, good idea," the thin man dug a card out of his own pocket. "Same here."

Geez, she practically had them falling all over themselves to help her. Did she have some magic charm in her pocket or something?

"I don't have a card with me," the last guy said, "But I'll give you my number."

Thelma jotted it down in her little notebook, and the guys hurried out the door.

"How was that for some good detective work?" Thelma was grinning triumphantly.

"Pretty good," I admitted.

"Coworkers are always willing to gossip, especially if they think you have information to share in exchange."

"What information did you have to share?"

"Well, none, really, but I maybe hinted that as a private detective I had access to some insider's stuff... "

"Boy, I wish I could lie like you do," I laughed.

"Hey, I didn't lie! I told you, I *hinted*."

"Right. Anyway, their suspicions gave me an idea."

"Let's hear it." Jack prompted me when I paused.

"Think about what we know so far. Michelle believes – or at least, she says she does – that Bill is on the road two weeks out of the month. But according to his boss, that isn't true. He only needs to make one overnight trip per month for the company meeting, all of his other work is done remotely. The thing is, he must be working during those two weeks, so he must have a second office somewhere."

Jack nodded. "Good point, Rainie. So what are you thinking, that he has a girlfriend he stays with?"

"And maybe that girlfriend is in Terre Haute…" Thelma added.

"Right. So if this turns out to be the case, what are we thinking? That Michelle found out about his girlfriend, followed him to his gym and shot him?"

223

"I know I'd consider shooting a guy for cheating on me," Thelma grinned. "But only if I was sure I could get away with it. I wouldn't want to do jail time over scum like that."

"Michelle had twice the motive," Jack pointed out. "Her anger over Bill cheating, and her desire to have him out of the way so she could be with Riley."

"It doesn't seem fair for her to be angry with Bill when she was doing the same thing." I protested.

"Fair? I don't think she was thinking about fairness. Or much else, frankly. You have to be pretty much out of your head with fury to kill someone, unless you're a psychopath, and I don't think Michelle fits that profile."

"The whole scenario seems so... trite." I shook my head. "Like something written for a TV movie."

"Hey, not every case is going to be strange or unusual, Rainie. Stereotypes develop for a reason."

"So what's our next step? How do we figure out if Bill had a girlfriend? It doesn't seem like anyone knew him well enough for him to confide in."

"There are other ways. If Bill was spending half his life in Terre Haute, he had to have left a trace of some kind."

Jack's phone started buzzing. "Hang on." He answered it, and Thelma and I fell silent while he talked.

"Not great timing, Harry. I'm in Indy... yeah, I'm helping Rainie with a thing. It'll take me three hours to get back to town... yeah..." he listened for a long minute. "Okay, yeah, I can do that. No, Rainie can drive the car back... I'll be there in thirty."

He disconnected. "Sorry, ladies, but I have to go; Harry needs me to fly to Ohio. I need you to drop me off at the airport, and you can take Eddie's car home."

"Wow, really?" Thelma was grinning happily. "Some hot case you're on?"

"I just need to help Hopper grab a guy." Jack was already heading for the door, and Thelma and I hurried to catch up. "Harry is arranging a flight with a guy he knows. I need to get there in a hurry."

"Hopper is back to work?" I was surprised; he'd been in a pretty serious car wreck just a few weeks ago.

"Part time, and on crutches. He ran down the guys whereabouts, but he needs me to actually take physical custody of him."

We were piling into the car. "I'll drive to the airport. You can just leave Eddie's car at your house, he can pick it up."

"Okay, but what about Bill? What should I do next?"

"Get online, try searching his name and Terre Haute."

"We can search other towns nearby too," Thelma suggested. "That guy was just guessing about Terre Haute."

"Good thinking," Jack approved. "Get what info you can. I won't be gone long, probably just overnight."

We dropped him at the airport and headed for home, the music cranked. I was enjoying the drive; Eddie's car was big and powerful, and so well balanced it almost seemed to drive itself. I know I was being a bit disloyal to my faithful old Escort, but the truth is, the Charger was so different it was almost like a different species. Like comparing dogs to cats: once you got past the fact they both had four legs and a tail, there weren't many similarities.

All in all, I felt pretty good about the trip. Nothing had gone wrong, and I felt like we had actually made some progress. Maybe we could keep Riley out of jail after all.

# Chapter Ten

We got back to town, and Thelma finally turned the music down. "So, you want to use my computer to do the research?"

"To tell you the truth, I think I might put it off until tomorrow," I admitted, feeling a little guilty. "I need to take a walk; I've had enough sitting for one day."

"Uh oh, wanting a smoke, huh?"

"Yeah." I sighed. How long would the cigarettes seem like such a focal point in my life?

"I'll walk with you if you want. We can hike the McCoy Creek trail, maybe stop and play in the water."

I laughed. "Sure why not?"

That's another thing I loved about Thelma. If you ever asked her about "age appropriate activities" she would probably look at you as if you were speaking a foreign language. I really wish I could learn her live-in-the-moment philosophy.

I dropped Thelma off just as the sun

was going down and headed for home. It had been a long day, and I was eager to take a hot bath and crawl into bed.

I parked Eddie's car in front of my house, and gave it a loving pat before I walked away from it. I called to tell him where it was, but his phone went straight to voicemail. I left him a message and called it a night.

I didn't get around to working Riley's case Wednesday. My morning started with my mother calling me all in a tizzy; someone had broken into her greenhouse and stolen all of her marijuana plants. That wasn't the part that had her upset, though; she could grow more pot, but whoever had broken in had also vandalized the place, smashing all the tables and knocking over all of her other plants.

"Who would do this?" My mother was in tears, standing at the door of the wrecked greenhouse. "Just look what they've done!" She knelt in the mess and picked up a broken tomato plant. "This was just... vicious!"

"I don't know, Mom," I shook my head at the mess. "Did you report it to the police?"

"Of course not!" She looked aghast at the suggestion. "Why would I do that?"

"Mom, someone broke in, they vandalized your property..."

"And stole marijuana plants that I am responsible for!" She pointed out. "Do you know how many hoops I had to jump through to get a license to grow? I thought I had it secured... but if the state finds out someone broke in they might revoke my license."

"I'm sure you aren't the first person this has happened to, but... I guess I see your point. Okay, I'll help you clean it up, and we'll think of some way to secure it better."

"Cameras." I heard my brother Jason's voice and turned to him with a wan smile. Mom had called out the troops; I wondered if my sister Brenda would turn up next.

"Hey, Jason."

"Hi." He stood in the doorway, hands on hips, and shook his head in disgust. "Crazy people. But you already have a good fence, and locks on the doors. But face it, it's a greenhouse, all glass. They could just as easily break a window. We'd better install some security cameras."

"I hate cameras!" My mother fretted.

"I know, Mom, but you will be the only one who can access them."

"How do you know? People hack into that stuff all the time."

"Trust me, Mom. I'll make sure it's secure."

Mom looked dubious, but then Jason literally rolled up his sleeves and grabbed a broom, changing the subject. "Come on, let's get this cleaned up."

It took most of the day to get everything straightened up. Mom insisted on rescuing every plant, carefully repotting every living root. Jedediah fixed the door, and Jason again mentioned cameras, but without a computer, we couldn't figure out a way for Mom to use one.

"We'll have to find some old school cameras," Jason said. "The kind that record on a VCR. I'll look on eBay and find you one."

"All right," Mom sighed and locked the door. "I hate that it's even necessary."

"I know, Mom." I hugged her tight. She hated reminders that it wasn't just the government out to get you. She would prefer to believe there was good in everyone.

"I won't have to worry for a while, anyway. No one is likely to break in to steal tomato plants."

I took my leave of her and headed home.

Eddie's car was gone, but Jack's truck was parked in front of my house when I got home. Jack himself was parked on my porch, his long legs sprawled out in front of him. He had a bottle of beer in his hand, a rare sight, and I saw a paper bag at his feet, just about the right size to hold a twelve pack. Well, this was interesting.

"Hey."

"Hey." He sounded different this evening, a little down, maybe even dispirited. He smiled at me, and I immediately thought of Eddie: it was one of those smiles that didn't reach the eyes.

"You okay?"

"Sure."

"Come on in. You can put the rest of your beer in the fridge."

He followed me in, silently sipping his beer as he watched me let George out and grab his food dish. In the kitchen he pulled out two empties from the twelve pack of Sam Adams and put them in my recycling bin. He stuck the rest in the fridge, keeping two out. He popped one open and handed it to me.

I had no idea what was wrong with him, but I figured the best thing to do was just go with it. I accepted the beer, took a sip, then set about making George's dinner.

"Are you hungry?" I asked.

"Not really. Besides, I don't care much for peanut butter with beer." He smiled when he said it, and I saw a shadow of his usual humor, but it faded quickly.

"I could order pizza."

"Nah. I'm good." He took another long drink of his beer.

I took George his dinner. He was basking under his light, his head raised and his eyes closed, looking regal. In more whimsical moods I had considered making a little paper crown to put on his head when he was sitting like that, but fortunately for the iguana's dignity I'd never actually given in to the urge.

Back in the kitchen Jack was sitting at the counter, rolling his fresh beer between his palms. I sat on the stool next to him.

"Did you have a rough day?" I asked him just to have something to say. He gave me that little not-quite-a-smile again.

"Something like that."

He went back to staring at his beer, and I let it go.

He took another long pull on his beer and set it down, not taking his eyes off of it, so that when at last he spoke it seemed he was talking to the picture of Sam Adams on the label.

"A friend of mine died today."

"I'm sorry to hear that." I put a hand on his arm, and he laid his hand over mine, hanging on as if it meant something.

"He was with me... well, during some tough times, back in the day. We joined the service together, went through ops training at the same time."

"Does Eddie know him?"

"They've met, but Steve was on his way out by the time Eddie and I teamed up."

"On his way out?"

"He'd had enough, didn't do the last two years with me." Jack took another long swallow of his beer. It was almost empty, and he held it, staring at it for a long moment like it had some hidden meaning.

"Want another?"

"I'll get it." He got up, finishing the last of his. "How about you?"

"Not ready yet." I held up my half-finished beer. He rinsed his empty out and carried it back to the bin, still efficient Jack even in his sorrow, and grabbed a fresh one.

"You know, not everyone can handle what we do. Did." Jack shook his head. "Special Forces, I mean. We were working for the good of the country, we knew that, but sometimes…"

He shook his head again and stared out the window, his eyes unfocused. I thought again of Eddie, of the lost look he so often had, of his brilliant smile that so seldom met his eyes. It wasn't a look I'd seen on Jack before. I had always thought he was too bold, too balls-to-the-wall out there to be bothered by whatever had affected Eddie. Obviously, that wasn't the case. I wanted to go to him, comfort him somehow, but I could tell by his stiff posture a touch would not be welcomed. I waited him out.

"So anyway, this morning Steve shot himself."

He said it in a tone like, "so anyway, Steve went to the store." But I could hear what lay underneath the matter-of-fact cadence, an ever-so-slight tremble in his voice that threatened to break my heart. I took a step toward him, but suddenly he set his beer in the sink and walked away.

"Sorry to bother you, Rainie. I've got to go."

I hurried to catch up with him.

"Wait, Jack." I grabbed his arm just as he reached the front door and he turned to me. "Why don't you hang out for a while?" I didn't think he was drunk, but I thought his emotional impairment might be as much of a danger on the road.

He stared at me, his eyes so dark and filled with pain I felt tears prick the back of my own eyes. I reached up and put a hand on his cheek.

"Please. Stay with me for a while."

He put his own hand over mine, still staring at me, seeming to be searching for something in my face.

"You're a good friend, Rainie."

He leaned toward me, and I expected a light kiss on the forehead, but what I got was his lips pressed to mine. His arms went around me and the kiss deepened. For once in my life I didn't feel a need to analyze the kiss. I didn't care who was the aggressor or what it all meant. I just gave myself over to it, and that familiar fluttering in my tummy spread through all of me, a not-unpleasant thrill of excitement, almost like the sensation I got when I topped the first hill on a roller coaster.

I could feel his arousal pressing into my belly, and that made me lean into him harder. I'd heard of this sort of thing before; a lot of people reacted to death with a need for lovemaking. I understand it's some sort of survival instinct, a reaffirmation of life going on, and it's fairly common.

But frankly, at the moment I didn't care about the psychology of it; I only cared that he not stop. My whole body was tingling, as if a million tiny fingers were running over every inch of my skin, coaxing every nerve in my body awake. I was hyper aware of every sensation: his hands on my back, his breath on my cheek, his beard stubble against my chin, the heat of his body pressed to mine and the rippling muscles on his back where my hands rested.

His hands slid down my back to my thighs and he lifted me, pulling my legs around his waist and pushing me back against the door. His lips travelled to my neck, to my favorite spot just below my ear. When he spoke his voice was rough.

"Please don't tell me 'no' this time."
No? What the hell was that: 'no?' I

couldn't have told him that if there was a gun to my head, not when every nerve ending in my body was screaming "Yes! Yes! Yes!" I couldn't seem to say it, so instead I just tightened my legs around him. I guess that was answer enough; he pulled me away from the door and carried me to the bedroom.

He sat on the edge of the bed with me on his lap and pulled my shirt over my head. His beard stubble was rough on my neck and then he had my bra off and he was nuzzling my breasts. The warmth in my belly had turned to liquid fire and I pulled at his shirt. I wanted to feel naked skin, I wanted – no, I needed – to have him pressed against me.

Abruptly he pushed me off of him and we were both on our feet, and he unzipped my skirt and it fell to the floor in a gauzy puddle. I went to work on his belt, and there were a few moments of awkward fumbling. Finally we were both naked and he pushed me back on the bed. I had a brief moment of panic at the thought of visible cellulite, but then his hands were on me and the ability to think coherently abandoned me.

What happened next is too private to relate, so you'll just have to figure it out for yourself. I will give this one critique though: "wow!"

Eventually we both fell asleep. I woke

up once, just as dawn was lighting the window, to find Jack sprawled across the other side of the bed, one hand on my thigh. I had a moment of wondering what the hell had come over me, and then sleep took me down again.

When I woke up again it was to the blare of my alarm, and Jack was gone. I threw on an over-sized t shirt and stumbled to the kitchen for coffee. There was a coffee cup, freshly washed, overturned in the sink, and a note in front of the coffee maker.
"Had to be in Warsaw by 8 am. I'll call you."
Well, at least there was a note. I had expected there to be no sign at all that Jack had been there, as if I'd only dreamed he'd been in my bed last night. I sat and drank my coffee at the counter, mentally kicking myself. It had seemed so right last night, but what had I been thinking?
Well, that was a dumb question. Obviously I hadn't been thinking at all.
Now I suppose Jack will call, we'll have some awkward conversation, and then I'll probably never see him again.
Damn. I was going to miss the wild adventure, the flirting… oh hell, I would miss everything about him.
Oh well, I'm a big girl, I'll get over it. I went to get dressed and headed for Thelma's.

It was raining again, the sky that certain gray shade that you just knew meant a full day of rain with no let up. Terrific. Just what I needed.

Thelma picked up on my mood within minutes.

"Uh oh, what's wrong?"

"Nothing I want to talk about."

"Not even to me?"

"Not even to my mother's dog."

Thelma laughed. "Must be embarrassing, huh? What, did you come out of a public restroom with your skirt stuck in your pantyhose?"

I smiled. "I don't wear pantyhose."

"Good point. So what is it? Toilet paper on the shoe? Or did you leave home with your shirt inside out again?"

"I wish." I took a deep breath, knowing there was no use. This wasn't a secret I could keep from Thelma. "I slept with Jack last night."

"What? Holy shit, are you kidding me?"

"Afraid not."

"So why so glum? Rainie, this is great news! How was it?"

"Thelma!" I blushed. "That's hardly the point!"

"Then what is?"

"Jack and I… we had kind of a good

thing going, you know? But now it'll probably be all weird. Hell, he'll probably never even call me again."

"Don't be ridiculous! I keep telling you he's got a real thing for you."

"Yeah, well he didn't say good bye this morning, just left me a short note."

"Maybe he had some place to be."

"He did." I briefly filled her in on Steve's suicide and why Jack went to Warsaw.

"Well, that is a shame." Thelma clucked her tongue. "So many young men lost to wars, even long after the fighting is over. The thing is, he obviously didn't ditch you."

"Still, it's probably going to be awkward from here on out."

"Only if you let it be. Just relax, let it play out. You worry too much over things you should be enjoying."

"I know." And I did know that was true. Didn't stop me from doing it, though.

I was just saying good bye to Thelma at four o'clock when my phone started playing "Flirting With Disaster."

"There you go," Thelma grinned. "Told you he wasn't ditching you."

I stared at my phone, reluctant to answer it.

"Answer it!" Thelma urged. "Don't be such a chicken."

I took a deep breath and hit the button to accept the call. "Hey."

"Hey yourself." Jack still sounded subdued. "I'm sorry I took off like that this morning. I woke up late, and I promised Emily I'd be here early."

"That's okay," I lied. I wondered who Emily was. As if reading my thoughts over the phone, he told me.

"Emily is Steve's little sister. She's a real mess, Rainie. I wish I'd brought you with me. You know how to handle grief."

I didn't know what to say to that. I guess I'd handled his grief, all right.

"I'm going to have to stay down here for a couple of days. There's not going to be a funeral, but Emily needs some support. She's all he had… " Jack broke off, and I heard him swallow. I could almost feel his grief, as if it were being transmitted from cell tower to cell tower all the way from Warsaw.

"Do you want me to come down?" I offered. He was silent for a moment, and when he finally spoke I could hear the reluctance in his voice.

"No, I'll be okay." I heard his deep intake of air, like a sigh in reverse, and when he spoke again his tone was louder, stronger… the voice of Jack in tight control.

"Listen, you remember that mess with Smitty?"

Smitty was a friend of Jack's, a big guy with a big heart. A few weeks ago his ex-girlfriend had been badly beaten, and she had accused Smitty of doing it. The thing is, Smitty vehemently denies it, and what's more, I suspected she had done the damage to herself in an attempt to get him thrown in jail. We had found some evidence to that effect, but in the meantime Smitty was still under the gun. He had taken to documenting his whereabouts at all times, even putting cameras all over his house, in case she tried it again.

"Sure. I thought they were going to drop the charges."

"We thought so, but it seems someone beat up Shantelle again."

"What? No way!"

"Yeah, and this time she's in the hospital. They arrested Smitty, and he called me, asking if I could bail him out, but... well, I really can't leave here right now."

"I know. What can I do?"

"This is a huge favor to ask, but could you do it? I have cash out at my place; you just have to take it up to St. Joe to the jail and get him out."

"Oh boy."

"I know, it's a lot to ask. I can try Eddie again, but he wasn't answering his phone."

"No, that's fine. I'll be happy to do it."

"Okay, the money is in the kitchen.

There's a false wall in the back of the cupboard over the sink. You'll need five thousand."

"Okay," I said. I didn't say what else I was thinking, which was: why in the world did he feel a need to keep that much cash around? Maybe he bailed people out on a daily basis.

"There's a key box on the door. You have a pen? I'll give you the combination for that and the alarm code."

"Okay." I dug my notebook out of my purse and wrote the numbers down.

"Just be sure you get that alarm code in fast. You only have two minutes before it goes off."

"I can handle it. But... I've never bailed anyone out before."

"They'll lead you through it. Just go in through the main door at the courthouse and tell them what you need to do."

"All right, I'll take care of it."

"Thanks, Rainie. I really appreciate it. I should be back Saturday night, I'll stop by then, okay?"

"Sure." That was nice. I had half expected to be dumped by phone. "I'll be here."

"I know, babe, you always have been."

With that he disconnected, leaving me with a strangely warm feeling. I began to suspect maybe I wasn't going to get dumped after all.

Thelma grinned at me. "There, that wasn't so awkward, was it?"

"No, I guess not."

"See? Quit fighting it and just let yourself fall in love with the guy already."

"Whoa! Hang on a minute! I have no intention of falling in love. That's just all around a bad idea."

"Oh yeah, and your succession of casual relationships has worked out so well."

"That's the point. I thought I had something with Michael, and look how tenuous that turned out to be."

"This is different. I can tell by the look on your face when you talk about Jack."

"Look, the whole falling in love thing is dumb. It's like the difference between renting and buying a house. If you rent and later decide the house is unsuitable for whatever reason you can go find another one, no hard feelings. But if you buy a house, that's a whole new level of commitment, a whole different set of complications to untangle yourself from."

"Oh honey, you're over thinking this! Falling in love is supposed to be just what it sounds like. Let yourself go and just fall!"

"Sounds like a great way to break your neck."

Thelma laughed. "Not with those big, strong arms to catch you!"

I rolled my eyes at her. "I'd rather

depend on my own strong arms, thank you!"

"Oh Rainie, I despair ever finding the romantic in you. So what did he want, anyway?"

I didn't want to tell her about bailing Smitty out; she would want to come with me, and I was feeling a need to be alone. "He said he'd see me Saturday when he got home."

"Hah! And you thought he was going to dump you. I told you girl, he's got it bad for you."

"Well, we'll see about that. Anyway, I need to get home. I'll talk to you tomorrow."

# Chapter Eleven

**I** scooted over to Niles and down the winding road to Jack's place. He had a couple of nice acres, isolated from his neighbors but not so far out of town that it was inconvenient.

I pulled into the driveway. The property was a mess right now with the construction going on. There were deep ruts running through the grass where heavy trucks had come and gone from the site of the new house, and even the asphalt driveway had taken a beating from the unaccustomed weight. I could see a couple of pickup trucks still parked by the new building, a couple of dedicated workers staying on the job until the five o'clock quit time.

I went slow, bumping over a couple of potholes, and shortly drove off the asphalt onto a temporary dirt driveway that led to Jack's trailer, as far from the construction mess as he could put it.

The trailer was used but well-maintained, white with light blue shutters. There was a simple set of fiberglass steps leading up to the front and back doors; he didn't intend to be living in it long enough for anything more permanent.

I stopped my Escort on the gravel pad designated for parking and walked around to the back, digging my notebook out of my purse as I went. First I needed the code for the key box, then the one to shut off the alarm.

Hopper once told me that private investigators must learn certain skills to be effective. One of the most important is to be observant, to take in the details of your surroundings, because you never knew what smallest detail would be relevant to the case you're working on. Besides, such awareness prevents men with nefarious motives from sneaking up on you.

I'm still new to the PI thing. My skills are far from the honed tools of the trade that Hopper and Jack employ. That's why I was too intent on the search for my notebook, and didn't see the man hiding behind the shed until he was racing across the short distance between it and me.

I looked up, startled, but too late to prevent him from grabbing me and spinning me around. He hooked one arm around my neck and under my left arm.

"Hey!" I tried to twist away, but his grip was too strong.

"What the hell are you doing?" A

second guy came from around the back of the shed. "That isn't Jones!"

"I know!" The guy holding me grunted. I hadn't managed to break away, but at least I was making him work to keep a hold on me. "Help me with her!"

Jack and Eddie had both taught me some simple self-defense techniques, and drilled me on them in the hopes they would become instinctual. I don't know that I'd gotten to that point yet, but with adrenalin kicking in like an intravenous shot of espresso, I fought back.

The second guy was coming at me from the front, not looking too happy about it. I was hoping to make him regret his choice even more. I grabbed onto the first guy's arm like a chin-up bar and kicked out at the second guy.

Jack and Eddie had both told me not to hesitate to kick a male attacker between the legs; although there was always the possibility they would just grab my foot and throw me to the ground, the mere threat of injury to those most sensitive man parts would make most attackers hesitate, and a good shot could put him down long enough for me to run. I had asked Jack if he would ever stoop to a below-the-belt attack.

"It might not be very macho or gentlemanly, but if it's his balls or my life, you're damned straight I would."

So there it was: if it was good enough for Jack, it was good enough for me. I kicked as hard as I could, wishing I was wearing steel-toed boots but hoping even the stiff end of my sandal would do the job if I put enough force behind it.

I made a solid connection, and the guy made a sound somewhere between a gush of air, a moan and a curse. He clamped his hands over his crotch and dropped to his knees, his face draining to pale. He had a patch over one eye, and that absurd little voice in my head shouted :"Aye, matey, there's one in the hull fer ya!" I had a strange urge to laugh, but really, there was no time for that.

I had dropped my purse, but I still had my keys in my left hand. I swung my arm up, hoping to gouge something tender on the guy holding me. The move was awkward, but I hit something; the guy yelped and his grip loosened. I ducked from under his arm and got the keys in my right hand, fumbling for the tiny bottle of pepper spray attached to the key ring.

I'd never actually used it, but I had studied it in detail; I managed to flick the safety catch off of it and got my finger on the spray button before the one I'd kicked pushed himself to his feet with a cry of rage. He lunged at me and I pointed the little canister and let go with a long blast.

He screamed and clamped his hands over his eyes, but unfortunately I had held the pepper spray too close to myself; I felt the little droplets hit my cheeks and a second later I was crying out, my eyes burning and tearing. I turned away blindly, setting my feet to run, but the first guy had already recovered from what little damage my kick had caused and he grabbed me again. He body slammed me to the ground and dropped onto my back with both knees; I would have cried out in pain, but all I could manage was an *oof* when the air was forced out of my lungs.

"Hang on to her 'til I get some rope or something!" The first guy ordered his partner.

"Not 'less you tell me what the hell you're doing! This ain't part of the plan!"

"I'm tired of waiting for Jones to show up. This is his girlfriend; we can use her to get him to come to us."

"This chick?" The partner looked down at me. "Are you sure?"

The man had my hands pinned behind my back, but he was breathing hard; I was twisting and bucking, and the effort of restraining me was taking a toll. Not so much that I really had much hope of getting away, but I wasn't going to stop trying.

"Hell yes, I'm sure!" the guy was moving toward the shed, in search of rope, I assumed.

I couldn't believe I was going to be kidnapped again. What the hell was I, a PI or a professional kidnap victim?

"Jack is going to kill you for this!" I gasped defiantly.

"Not if we kill him first." The guy jerked on my arms, forcing a cry of pain from me. "Now shut the hell up and hold still!"

"Hell no!" I twisted one leg under me and pushed hard, putting everything I had into it, and shoved hard. The maneuver partially dislodged him and he let go of my arms. I hurriedly scrambled to my knees, and almost made it to my feet before he punched me hard on the side of the head. I slipped away into unthinking blackness.

It wasn't long before I had reason to believe that *un*thinking blackness was one hell of a lot better than *conscious* blackness. I came to in total darkness, and at first I thought I must be blindfolded. I tried to lift a hand to take the cloth off my eyes, but my hands were taped behind my back. As if that wasn't bad enough, my feet were taped together!

"Oh no. Oh no, no, no…" I was saying it, but my mouth was covered with duct tape, so all that came out was "nnn…nnn…" I struggled to sit up, panic already rising up in me. My claustrophobia extended to being tied; that feeling of helplessness, that inability to ward off even the mildest of attacks, induced wild terror in me.

I twisted to the side and got my back against a wall and pushed myself into a sitting position. I stretched my legs out in front of me…or tried to, at any rate. My knees were still bent when I made contact with another wall.

What the hell! They had bound me, gagged me, and stuffed me in…what? Where the hell was I? I couldn't breathe!

I braced my feet against the wall and shoved and slid my back up the wall. There was enough room for me to stand up, at least. I threw myself to the right and almost immediately ran into another wall. Sobbing, I went left, and ran into a wall after only a few rapid hops. Okay, at least I could move around a little. That was something, right?

No, it wasn't *anything*. It was no comfort at all!

There was no air in this tiny space; they must have sealed it off, made it as airtight as a vertical coffin buried six feet under. I was suffocating!

"NNN!" I tried to scream, but nothing was coming out. I sobbed again, and felt tears spilling down my cheeks. Almost immediately my nose started to stuff up. No! I had to stop crying! With my mouth taped shut my nostrils were all I had.

*Get a grip, Rainie!* I mentally shouted at myself, but myself was busy freaking out and didn't listen to me. "NNNN! NNNN!" I kept trying to scream, but the tape was on tight, and now my nose was running, and I snuffled it back and it started to clog and I gagged and it occurred to me I was about to die, I was about to choke to death on my own vomit…

Wait, was that light?

Like a sudden shout penetrating the cacophony of my panic, I saw a thin line of light. I sucked in a breath through my nose and peered more closely.

Yes, there was a door in front of me, and on the other side there was dim light. I wasn't blindfolded after all! See, wasn't that something?

It wasn't much, but my terrified brain latched on to it. If light could penetrate, so could air. I stuck my face against the crack and breathed in. I remembered being locked in a shed, and that had been terrifying, but this place was so dark, so damned small…

The air coming in through the crack smelled musty and dank, and I wasn't getting as much as I wanted through my snot clogged nose, but it was air.

I breathed again and again, trying to soothe myself with that simple, life affirming action. It helped, a little, but I was still bound and gagged and locked in a closet. I needed out. Right now!

I kicked at the door, but it didn't have any give. Was it a steel core door? Was it deadbolted? I tried to hang on to those thoughts, logical ideas that might find me a way out, but they skittered away like cockroaches exposed to the light of my terror.

I sat down and braced my back against the wall and kicked at the door with both feet, giving it all I had, determined to break through it. I kicked and kicked, the whole time making that weird keening sound that was the only scream I could muster: "NNN! NNNN!"

"Hey! Knock it off in there!" A man's voice, from the other side of the door. His threat, rather than calming me, made me redouble my efforts.

"NNN! NNNN! NNNNNNN!"

"Hey! Goddammit!" Suddenly the door flew open and the big man was leaning over me. I blinked at the dim light but I was already struggling to get up, to run for the open door. "I said, knock it off!" He swung a meaty palm and caught me in the face and I fell against the back wall.

"What the hell is going on?" The other guy ran over.

"She's throwing some kind of fit." The first guy moved to close the door again and I stuck out my feet to stop him.

"NNN!" I was crying now, more

terrified than ever that they would shut the door. My nose was clogging again and I really couldn't breathe! I snorted desperately, trying to clear my nostrils, and gagged again.

"Christ, quit crying!" The second man said in disgust. "You're gonna choke on your own snot."

I already *knew* that, hell, I was practically an expert at this getting kidnapped stuff, and in fact, if I survived I might give classes on the subject, but that didn't mean I could stop the crying.

With a grimace the guy leaned over me and tore the tape off my mouth. It felt like it took six or seven layers of skin with it, but he could have peeled it down to the bone and I wouldn't have cared at that moment. I could breathe!

I took in a great whooping gasp of air, then another.

"All right, I'll leave it off for now, but you scream and I'll put it back on, you got it?"

I nodded, for the moment so grateful for the ability to breathe I wasn't even trying to get away.

"It's not like anyone can hear you anyway from down here, but I don't want to listen to any whining. Got it?"

I nodded again.

"Move your feet." He was trying to close the door again.

"No…please…"

"Get me the tape." He said to the other guy.

"NO! Not that…"

"Then move your goddamned feet!"

I had to pick the lesser of two evils. Reluctantly I pulled my feet back far enough for him to shut the door.

"Now keep quiet in there!'

Quiet, right. I felt a scream building up again when the door shut, blocking out all but that thin line of light. The scream was coming from somewhere way deep inside me, gathering in my chest and ready to make a run for my throat. I opened my mouth and forced myself to take a deep breath, swallowing the scream. I didn't want that tape back over my mouth.

What now? I pulled again at the tape on my wrists, but there was no give there. If I were flexible enough I might be able to bend over and chew the tape off my ankles, but I wasn't a contortionist, so not much hope there.

The line of light was thickest near the floor, which my panicky brain interpreted as the spot with the most air. I squirmed around and lay down with my mouth against the crack and concentrated for a while on breathing.

It didn't calm me much, but it helped a little. At least I no longer felt in danger of immediate suffocation. Now I just had that horrified, closed in feeling to deal with, the unreasonable fear that only a true phobia can produce. I was sure the wall was moving in behind me, coming closer and closer, while the ceiling inched its way toward me, so that soon I wouldn't be able to turn over, and shortly after that I wouldn't be able to move anything at all, and then the encroaching walls would press on my chest, compressing my lungs and slowly suffocating me...

I whimpered and abruptly sat up, needing to reassure myself that I still could. When I did my cheek scraped against something, and I cried out.

"Hey, shut up!" the man yelled at me, a reminder that he was still there and vigilant.

I rubbed my cheek against my shoulder and felt something wet. Great, I had cut myself. I would probably get blood poisoning and die a slow death...

Wait. I had cut myself! The message penetrated my terror: there was something sharp in here! If it cut my face, it could cut duct tape!

I scooted around until my back was to the door and pushed up against it. I used my finger tips to feel around for whatever had sliced my cheek. Finally I found it: a screw, improperly seated when the door frame was put in. It had missed the two-by-four, and the sharp end was sticking out, just a few inches above the floor.

Frantically I pushed my bound hands down on it and felt the point pierce the duct tape around my wrists. I jerked upward and was rewarded with the tiniest bit of give in the heavy tape. Yes! This would work!

With something constructive to do my panic quieted a bit, and I worked on the tape, trying to get as close to the edge with the screw as I could. It wasn't easy with my hands behind my back, but slowly I felt the tape giving a bit. I pulled my hands apart as much as I could, stretching the tape, and dug the tip of the screw in again. I was rewarded by a tiny tearing sound. The tape was giving way!

My triumph was short lived; it only tore a half inch or so. I was guessing there were probably several layers to cut through. Well, fine. I had time. I dug in again, stretched and pulled.

Somewhere in the back of my mind a thought was trying to form, something to the effect that my bound wrists were the least of my problems right now, but I concentrated on that tiny sharp point and refused to consider anything else. When faced with a mountain to move and nothing but a teaspoon to do it with, it was best to look at only the dirt within your immediate sight. To look up at the towering peak would be to give in to despair, and I didn't dare do that.

I poked and stretched, poked and stretched. I don't know how long I'd been at it before I became aware that I could hear the men talking in the other room. They were standing right outside the door. I scooted away from the screw. If they opened the door, I didn't want them to see what I was doing and take away my only hope for escape.

"She's right here," I heard one of them say, then there was a short pause. "All right, just ten seconds."

I heard a key turn in the lock and the door was wrenched open. One of the guys grabbed my hair and leaned in close to me. "Your boyfriend is on the phone," he sneered. "You got ten seconds to tell him you're okay, or you won't be. You got it?"

Not really; I couldn't get my terrified brain hang onto a coherent thought. My boyfriend? Who? But I nodded, wide-eyed. The other guy knelt in the doorway and stuck a cell phone close to my face.

"H-hello?"

"Rainie! I'm coming for you!"

"Jack…" I practically moaned his name. I felt so stupid, but I couldn't seem to say anything else. Just hearing his voice was strangely comforting, even without his promise of rescue.

The guy pulled the phone back and the other one slammed the door.

"That's it, proof of life. You have the money ready tomorrow by noon. We'll call and tell you where."

They ended the call and walked away. The return of the silence reminded me that I was still locked in a very tiny, very dark place. I scooted back to the wall and resumed chopping at the tape.

I worked at the tape until exhaustion overcame me, and I finally had to lie down. I did so with my mouth against the crack in the door, breathing deeply. I didn't know how long I'd been in here, but my stomach was growling, making me think that maybe it was nearing morning and breakfast time. I stayed on my side, concentrating on the freshet of air coming through the little crack, trying to shut off the sensation of encroaching walls. My heart was a painful throb in my chest, and I wondered just how long I could survive in this heightened state of terror.

I breathed and breathed and thought about Jack, out there somewhere, looking for me. If he found me, those guys were dead meat. I took some satisfaction in that, even if I was afraid he wouldn't find me until I'd already died of fright.

I breathed, and thought about Jack. I pictured him breaking in on my kidnappers and visiting all manner of violence on them.

He would more than kick their asses, he would demolish them, he would make them rue the day they had thought to take me. He would avenge every bruise and moment of terror I had suffered.

I'm not usually a violent person, but those particular fantasies were strangely comforting. Incredibly, I dozed off.

I had been buried alive! Stuffed in a pine box and covered with six feet of heavy clay soil, left to die and rot in the dark. But wait...I remembered my mom had promised to leave a string attached to a bell, so if I was buried by mistake I could ring it and Jack would come dig me up. I had to pull the string...but I couldn't. They had cut off my arms! Why did they do that? I squirmed around, searching for the string so I could pull it with my teeth... I had to let Jack know I was here, that I was alive! Where was the string? I had to find it...

I came awake abruptly, breathing hard, soaked in sweat, so disoriented that for a moment I thought the dream had been real, and I really had been buried alive.

A moment after that I let out a little sob of terror. It *had* been real, at least to a point. I remembered the kidnapping, remembered that I was bound and locked in a tiny closet. I felt another scream building in me, and I almost gave voice to it before I remembered the guy's threat, and the horror of having duct tape over my mouth. I released the scream in a pathetic mewl of terror and misery.

The sound of voices penetrated my panic, and I thought I heard someone say "Jack." I froze and listened, realizing it was my kidnappers again, not far away from the closet door.

"…you so sure he'll come for her."

"He'll come. Jerry says he's got it bad for her."

"What if he just sends someone else with the ransom?"

"He's too much a macho man for that. Trust me, his ego won't let him just pay up. He'll have to come in after her."

"Where are you setting up the drop?"

"Under the bridge up in Niles. We'll set it for after dark so there won't be any casual strollers around. As soon as he's in sight, you take the shot."

My heart seemed to stutter in my chest, and for a minute I found it hard to breathe again. Jack had laughed about these guys; he was disdainful of their incompetence. But this plan might just work! They were still talking, so I shut my inner voice up so I could listen.

"…don't get why we don't just kill her now."

"Because he'll probably insist on talking to her at least once more. After we set the drop you can do what you want with her."

"Probably strangle her. Don't want to fire a gun here."

"Either that or cut her throat. The mess won't matter."

"Might be quicker…"

I don't know if they were considering any other methods to do me in, because their voices faded from my hearing as they walked away. I swallowed hard. With my hands and feet tied they wouldn't find it a challenge no matter if they decided to strangle me or cut my throat. I hoped he used the knife; that would probably only hurt for a minute or so. Strangling would take a long time, and besides, it seemed so intimate….

What the hell was I thinking? Was I really deciding how I'd rather die instead of trying to get the hell out of here?

I struggled to a sitting position and pushed myself against the door, feeling around for the protruding screw. Once again the mountainous task of escape threatened to loom up and overwhelm me, but I pushed it aside and punctured the tape with the sharp tip. Stretch the tape, puncture, pull. Stretch, puncture, pull. I worked at it like a machine, not letting any other thought intrude, giving every ounce of my energy to the tedious task. Stretch, puncture, pull. Again and again.

And then it happened. I pulled my

hands apart to stretch the tape, and there was a final rip, and my hands were free!

I laughed and sobbed at the same time, holding my hands up in front of my face, wiggling my fingers, which were no more than slightly darker patches moving in the dark.

"I did it!" I whispered triumphantly and impulsively kissed my numb fingers, incredibly pleased with myself.

Until I remembered that my feet were still taped. And there was still a solid, locked door, and two very mean, armed men guarding it.

My spirits were dampened, but not quenched. *Remember, don't look at the mountain!* I reminded myself. *Just take your little spoon and keep digging!*

I bent down and worked at the tape around my ankles, suddenly realizing I was barefoot. That pissed me off; where were my sandals? I really liked them, they had thin soles, easy to slip on and off...

Once again I told my inner voice to shut up and let me focus. I picked at the tape until I found a loose end and carefully started peeling it away. At some point I had started crying again, but I didn't admonish myself this time. I just sobbed quietly and picked and pulled at the tape. Layer by layer I worked it, until finally I stripped the last bit away.

Okay, this was good. Very good. My

hands and feet were free.

I sat with my back against the wall and braced my feet against the door. I pushed as hard as I could, hoping for even a little bit of give.

Nope, not a bit.

The situation called for cool, clearheaded thinking. I had to come up with something clever, a way to pick the lock or signal for help.

But unfortunately I was locked in a miniscule closet and a man was planning to slit my throat before going off to Niles to shoot Jack. I had no capacity left for cool, clever thinking, so I was just going to have to be direct and brutal.

I kicked at the door, once, twice, three times. It didn't budge. I kicked harder, the terror welling up in me, and I forgot all about being quiet and started *snarling* at the door, cursing it, calling it every dirty name I could think of and inventing new ones when my blue vocabulary ran short.

"*Son* of a *bitching* door, *open*, damn it!" I kicked with one foot, then the other, then both at the same time, my fear giving way to a bit of rage, fueled in part by hysteria. I kicked and kicked, my bare feet sliding against the varnished wood now and then, having little effect. I didn't wonder until much later why my kidnappers didn't come running at all the racket I was making; I just kept kicking and swearing. I wanted out!

I kicked up at an angle, and my foot hit the doorknob. It rattled, the first reaction I'd gotten, so I kicked it again and then again…

And suddenly the doorknob broke loose and went flying over my head, smacking the back wall of the closet before landing with a clatter next to me. The door flew open and hit the wall behind it with another clatter.

Stunned, I stared at the opening for what felt like a whole minute but was probably no more than three seconds. I got to my feet and lurched out of my little prison, expecting to see my captors racing in to stop me.

## Chapter Twelve

The room I staggered out to was huge and dimly lit. I saw boxes. Stacks and stacks of them running off as far as the dim light allowed me to see, piled high on industrial metal shelving that towered up into darkness. Just to the left were two folding chairs with a box between them, holding an overflowing ashtray and several foam coffee cups. For a few seconds I stared almost hungrily at the ashtray. A cigarette... if ever I had felt the need for my addiction's comfort, this was it...

Okay, forget that, there was no time to waste. I went to the right, looking for an exit.

I got to the end of the huge shelving unit, but it was only another aisle. The shelving continued after about eight feet. I looked to the right and left, and saw nothing but more shelves and darkness.

The place was laid out like a maze, the aisles twisting back on themselves, as if it were laid out by a demented minotaur instead of a merchant of novelties. Maybe they did this on purpose so the employees could amuse themselves on the overnight shift, playing hide and seek among the merchandise. If so, it would be an interesting employee perk, one that might make me want a job here.

I heard voices, and froze. Damn it, were they coming back so soon?

But no, the voices were getting fainter...

Abruptly, the lights went out, leaving me in complete darkness.

"Please... " I couldn't help a tiny sob of desperation. Which way was out?

I stood still, one hand on a wall of boxes next to me to keep myself oriented. I listened carefully for movement, but there was nothing. They must have left, shutting off the lights on the way out, thinking I was still bound and secure in the closet. That part was good, but how was I supposed to find my way out?

Okay, there should be lighted exit signs; they were required in any commercial building, and worked on separate circuits to the main lights, usually battery operated in case of power outages. All I had to do was find my way to the end of a main aisle and look both ways, and I would likely find an exit.

I moved forward slowly, my steps tentative, unsure what might be on the floor. I kept one hand trailing on the boxes for security. I walked for what seemed an hour, but I knew time was distorted here in the absolute darkness. It was almost like a sensory deprivation chamber, and I was craving light and noise like a diabetic craves sugar.

My brain was frantically searching for visual cues to orient me, but of course, there were none. The warehouse was absolutely silent, only the occasional whisper of my bare feet on the gritty concrete marking the passage of life; the acoustics were strange, and it sounded like the footsteps were coming from behind me, causing me to freeze in panic every few seconds.

I tried humming a little tune, thinking the sound would help, but instead it freaked me out. With nothing to reference it to it seemed like it was coming from someone else lurking there in the dark. I shut up and froze for a minute, just to confirm I was alone here.

Silence. Darkness. Now I could hear my own respirations, and again it seemed to be coming from somewhere behind me. The flesh on my neck tried to crawl up my scalp, and I shuddered and moved on.

Finally I reached the end of the row of boxes I was following. I stopped when my hand felt empty air and leaned forward cautiously, peering first left and then right.

Absolute darkness. Absolute silence.

I swallowed a growing sense of panic. There was nothing to be afraid of here! So it was dark, big deal! I wasn't afraid of the dark, or at least, I never had been before. I just needed to keep my wits about me and I would find the way out.

I stood there blinking, looking right and left, and finally saw a faint glow, like a candle in a window, miles distant. I didn't know if the bulb was going out, dimming with age, or if the sign was so covered in dust and grime that it acted like a shade, but I could just make out the "X" and the "T." Either it was an exit sign, or the doorway to excitement, and I seriously doubted that. I started for it in a stumbling run, quickly realizing what a bad idea that was in the pitch darkness. I tripped over something and went headfirst into a pile of cardboard boxes. They tumbled and fell around me, what seemed like hundreds of them, not particularly heavy but falling in an overwhelming avalanche. I was being buried alive... if I died in here, under a mountain of cardboard, would I eventually be recycled? That would certainly please my mother... well, except for that part where I would be dead...

I shut off that stupid little voice in my head, which as usual was not being of any use whatsoever, and thrashed my arms around, trying to clear a space overhead. I could move the boxes easily enough, but there were so many of them! I tried to move forward, but it was like cardboard quicksand, and every box I pushed out of the way was replaced by two or three more falling in.

I fell again, and this time stayed on my hands and knees, sobbing piteously, convinced I was going to die from the terror of this unending nightmare! I crawled forward, pushing the boxes out of my way with my head and occasionally my hands, moving in what I hoped was a steadily forward direction. Surely there had to be an end to them, there had to be a way out...

And then I was free of them, still surrounded by nearly total blackness, panting heavily on all fours on the cold concrete floor like a dog that had just run twenty miles in pursuit of its traveling master... but there in front of me, still impossibly far away, was that faintly glowing "X" and "T." I started for it, still crawling a few feet before the ache in my knees forced me back to my feet, and I shambled forward, sliding my feet, holding my arms in front of me like a bad actor playing at blindness, feeling for obstacles.

It seemed like I moved along that way for hours, the light never getting closer, as if it was receding into the distance at the same pace I was moving forward. But no, at last I could see I was getting nearer, the "E" and the "I" now showing faintly... definitely an exit sign, but now I wondered if the door would open? Surely if the sign itself was so poorly maintained the door would be locked! It was against all fire regulations, but then, so was letting the sign itself get so crusty that it couldn't be read. I wondered how long it had been since this place had been inspected, or for that matter, how long it had been since anyone had been in it except for me and my kidnappers?

I couldn't keep up my slow pace. The panic was building in me again, intensifying the closer I got to possible freedom. I stopped shuffling and ran the last few yards for the exit, heedless of unseen obstacles, my eyes focused on that faint but promising light.

I smashed into the door full speed, my hip catching the release bar, and wonder of wonders, it functioned! There was a loud creak and suddenly my eyes were blinded not by utter darkness, but brilliant sunlight!

I stumbled and stopped, blinking in the harsh light, my eyes tearing from the unexpected assault. I was in a concrete stairwell leading up.

The door swung shut with a loud bang behind me, an urgent reminder that I wasn't out of danger yet.

I ran up the stairs, tripping and stumbling, half blinded. I finally reached the top and ran flat out, straight into the arms of... a zombie!

He was gruesome, his face covered in blood, one eye missing and gore trailing out of his mouth. I spun away only to run into another one, a bloody woman in a bridal gown with an ax buried in the tender flesh of her neck.

I stared in horror. There were dozens of zombies… hundreds! They were shambling down the street, arms raised, growling and moaning, seeking… what? Brains, of course! Human flesh!

How long had I been in that closet? Had the world ended while I was down there? Were all those movies actual prophetic visions of things to come?

No, not possible. My terror had obviously just pushed me over the edge into the abyss of insanity. My mind had cracked like an egg crushed under a boot heel.

Sobbing with renewed terror, wondering if I would ever wake, I turned away from the bride to find the groom, a cleaver buried in his skull, reaching out to grab me. It occurred to me to wonder, if I was insane, could I be aware of it? Would I know I'd gone crazy?

No, this must be a nightmare induced by sheer panic. I was still in the closet, the whole sequence of events from cutting the tape loose to kicking the doorknob off to running out the exit door nothing more than a vivid dream. Now my mind must be dredging up other terrors to distract me from the reality of being trapped…

The zombies were laughing.

And the groom looked concerned, his eyes warm and compassionate in spite of the blood coursing down his face. And now I could make out what he was saying.

"Hey, are you all right?"

"Someone call security…" The bride spoke clearly through bloody lips.

With profound relief I realized the zombies were fake. They were wearing costumes; frighteningly accurate costumes, but they were not *really* flesh eating undead.

"Ma'am, do you need help?"

This voice belonged to a thick-set man in a bright yellow t-shirt. The bold lettering on his chest read:

SECURITY
10th Annual
Zombie Walk

Of course, I'd heard about this! Undead movies were wildly popular, and the fans enjoyed dressing like zombies, but then where is a zombie to go? So people organized events like this one, usually to benefit charity, and the zombies got together and walked the city streets, or sometimes got together and did the zombie dance from Michael Jackson's *Thriller* video.

Great fun, I think, a bit of silliness in a world that often takes itself entirely too seriously. Pretty weird to stumble into unexpectedly, though!

"Ma'am?" the security guy prompted me, and belatedly I nodded.

"I'm okay." But was I? I was shaking so bad my teeth were chattering and my knees were wobbly. The wedding couple was still standing there, watching me, but the rest of the zombies were moving on, apparently oblivious to my drama.

"Hey, you'd better sit down." The security guy tried to lead me to the concrete ledge that surrounded the stairwell I'd so recently run up.

"N-no..." I stammered, my mind finally going back to the fact that I had just escaped from kidnappers, men that might be waiting just beyond that door for me to let my guard down.

"I'll call 911..."

"No! No, I want... I want... " What did I want? I wanted... Jack! Yes, that would be good. "I want to call Jack."

"Who's Jack? Your boyfriend?"

My boyfriend?

"Um... yeah... I guess." I know I probably sounded pretty stupid, but I also knew I was still pretty freaked out. I was having trouble keeping my thoughts in any sort of order. My mind kept wanting to race down random paths, but I couldn't let it run away. I needed to talk to Jack, to let him know I was safe, and that my kidnappers were planning to kill him.

I heard a siren start to wail a few blocks away. The zombies kept moving past, moaning and laughing and moaning some more.

The security guy handed me his phone and I stared at it stupidly. I didn't know Jack's number! It was programmed into my phone so all I had to do was click on his name.

I stared at the zombies shambling by in the bright sunshine. The wail of the siren was getting louder, and there was a strange ringing in my ears. Everything seemed surreal, and for a moment time seemed to slow down.

"What's the matter?" The security guard asked. His voice sounded hollow, as if it were coming from the other end of a long tube. "Ma'am? Are you going to pass out? You'd better sit down..."

Pass out? Yep, that's exactly what I was going to do. But I didn't have time for that!

I leaned over and put my hands on my knees and took in a sharp breath, then another, deeper one. The dizziness faded, and time seemed to snap back into its regular track.

I stood upright again.

"I don't know Jack's number. It's in my phone."

He nodded sympathetically. "I'm lost without mine."

The sirens had drawn near, and now I saw flashing lights coming up behind the gruesome conga line of zombies. I sighed. Someone must have called 911 after all. Who would have suspected that zombies would carry cell phones?

I handed the phone back to the guy. "I need a phone book."

"What?"

"I've got to go."

"Wait, the cops are here..."

"Yeah, I know, but I need to talk to Jack." I turned and joined the zombie march just as the cop ambled up to the security guard. I heard the guy talking, probably pointing me out, but I hadn't done anything wrong. I didn't think the cop would make much effort to follow me.

I wove in and out of bloody bodies, passing most of them (these were obviously old school zombies, the kind that shambled mindlessly and never, ever ran!) until we got a block or so away from the cop. I saw a restaurant up ahead, and I made my way over to it.

I stepped inside, blinking at the sudden darkness. A hostess hurried over to me. "Good afternoon, may I help you?"

There was no one else in the place. I wondered briefly what time it was.

"Can I borrow your phone?"

"Are you all right?" It occurred to me that I might be a bit disheveled after my stint in the closet. I didn't have time to explain.

"Yes, please, I just need to use a phone… and a phone book."

"Well… " She hesitated, looking back over her shoulder. There was no one there. "All right, come over here." She led me to the hostess station, a podium to the right of the door. She pulled a phone book out from a shelf underneath. "Just make it kind of quick, okay?" She looked toward the back of the restaurant again, probably expecting her manager to come out and give her hell.

I hurriedly looked up the number for B&E. I asked for Belinda.

"Hi Rainie, what's up?"

"I don't have time to explain. I need Jack's number."

Belinda, being the ultra cool cucumber she was, didn't argue. I heard her tap her computer keyboard and in a few seconds she rattled off the number. I picked up a pen from the podium and wrote it on the back of my hand.

"Thanks."

"Tell me later," she said before she disconnected.

I hurriedly dialed Jack's number.

"What?" He answered. His voice was deep and harsh and he managed to convey all kinds of rage in that one word.

"Jack, this is Rainie."

"Rainie! Are you all right?" I was gratified by the relief in his tone. "Where are you?"

In the background I heard a cry of pain. "Who was that?"

"Never mind him, where are you?" Jack demanded again.

"I'm safe, but you're in danger! Don't go to that meeting! They said it's about the ransom but it's really a trap…"

"I know!" Jack cut me off. I heard another cry of pain. "Hold on."

I heard Jack talking again, but he had the phone away from his face. "Knock it off, Eddie. Rainie's on the phone, she's okay."

"Where is she?"

"I'll find out if you two will just keep it down." He came back to me. "What the hell happened?"

"Eddie is there?"

"Rainie, please! Tell me what happened."

"They snatched me right from your driveway and stuck me in a closet!" I couldn't help a tiny sob when I said it; the memory, the sheer terror, was too fresh. It seemed to come flooding back all of a sudden. "I used a screw and I kicked at the door and there wasn't anyone so I got away but there were zombies and then the cops came…"

"Whoa! Slow down, Rainie!"

"I'm sorry, I was just so scared, and then I wanted to warn you but I don't have my phone and I had to get your number…"

"I have your phone."

"You have it? How?"

"We're here, where you were. Tell me where you are, we'll come get you."

"I'm in downtown South Bend, at a restaurant…" I looked around for the name, finally saw it on the front of a menu. "Mark's Restaurant."

"All right, we'll be there in about five minutes." I heard a grunt and another cry of pain in the background. "See you soon."

I hung up the phone and turned to find the hostess standing a few feet away, looking at me with some concern.

"Hey, are you sure you're okay?"

"I am now."

"Are you… I mean, that bruise, and the blood on your face… is that for real, or just really good zombie makeup?"

"What?" I touched my face and felt the swath of dried blood from where the screw had gouged my cheek. Now that she mentioned it, my eye socket was throbbing, and I dimly remembered the guy backhanding me. At the time my fear was doing a good job of overriding any pain.

"Oh, that. It's fake." I ducked my head, glad that the restaurant was dim. "Thanks for letting me use the phone."

I hesitated only a moment before asking her for another favor. "Hey, I don't suppose... I mean, do you smoke?"

"Yeah," she answered, looking a little embarrassed. Smoking was no longer the "cool" thing to do.

"I hate to ask, but I lost mine... can I bum one from you? I know that's a lot to ask... "

"No, not at all!" She pulled a pack out of her apron pocket. "Do you have a light?"

"No," I sighed, embarrassed. This was turning out to be a pain, but I really needed a cigarette.

She came outside with me and let me use her lighter, and with a little wave at my heartfelt thanks went back inside.

I moved a little ways down the sidewalk so she couldn't see me through the big front window and puffed furiously on the cigarette. People passing by looked at me oddly, but most gave me little more than a second passing glance. With the zombie walk in town bruised and bloody people were practically the norm, even smoking zombies not deserving of more than a glance.

I didn't have to stand there long. I heard an engine rev around the corner and a few seconds later Eddie's shiny black Charger rumbled up to the curb. Jack leapt out of the passenger side before it came to a complete stop, and he was across the sidewalk and I was safe, wrapped tightly in his arms.

Okay, I know. I'm a strong, independent woman and I don't *need* a man to take care of me.

That doesn't mean I don't *want* one to, at least once in a while.

The comforting didn't last long. Eddie tapped his horn impatiently.

"Come on, get in! We need to move!"

Without a word Jack led me to the car and directed me into the front seat. I slid in and scooted over next to Eddie to make room for Jack.

"Hey, good to see you." Eddie grinned, even his eyes brightening for a moment, and I laughed.

"There aren't w-words to tell you how h-happy I am to see you!" Suddenly I was shaking like one of those cheesy animated skeletons people hang up at Halloween, so much so that it was making my teeth chatter. Eddie squeezed my leg.

"You're okay, now."

But I wasn't, not really. As safe as I knew I was between these two solid, capable guys, my heart was still pounding painfully and I was afraid I was going to break into hysterical tears at any moment.

There was a muffled thump from behind us and I craned my neck to see if we'd been rear-ended.

"Don't worry about it." Eddie put the car in gear and took off. The thumping continued, and I wondered if there was something wrong with Eddie's car, but neither one of them seemed concerned. It took on an almost rhythmic quality, and I thought I heard muffled swearing. It sounded like… hm. It sounded like it did when I was trying to kick my way out of the closet.

"Is there someone in the trunk?" I finally asked.

"Yeah, one of the guys who took you. Duct-taped head to toe. He's fine; this baby has sixteen point one cubic feet of trunk space." Eddie laughed.

"Yeah, more space than he'd have in the average Japanese hotel room," Jack agreed with a grin.

"Why is he in the trunk?" I asked stupidly.

"We're going to take him some place private so he can tell us where his partner is."

I thought of the grunts and cries of pain I'd heard over the phone, and I grimaced, not so much for the pain inflicted on my kidnapper, but for the pain that was always reflected in Eddie's eyes. I hated the idea that he had to do something so cruel for my sake. I looked over at him, and he met my eyes briefly.

"Hey, sometimes I do this kind of work because I *want* to." He smiled, and I wondered if he'd read my mind.

"We're going to drop you off at Tommy's." Jack informed me.

"Tommy's? Why?"

"Because we have to finish this business, and we need you to be safe. Tommy is up to speed on the situation. He'll keep you safe."

"I don't need a babysitter!"

"Okay." Jack shrugged. "Eddie, drop her off at home."

Eddie looked over at Jack but didn't say anything. I sat quiet for a minute, surprised by how easily they had capitulated. I had expected an argument. Come to think of it, I think I'd hoped for an argument. I didn't want to go home and sit by myself; I was still a shaking, traumatized mess! What the hell were they thinking, just dropping me off all by myself?

I turned to glare at Jack, and he was grinning at me.

"Just kidding." He kissed me on the forehead. "Let Tommy bandage your cheek, and put some ice on your eye." He handed me my cell phone. "I'll call you as soon as we know something."

"You're a real jerk sometimes."

"I know. That's why you love me."

Eddie burst out laughing at that, and what could I say? It was at least partially true.

# Chapter Thirteen

Tommy's place was a cute little two story house with a big, well-manicured lawn. There were two bedrooms and a full bathroom upstairs, a living room, dining room, kitchen and half-bath downstairs. I sat on the closed toilet lid in the half-bath while he fussed over me with a first aid kit, washing out the deep scratch on my cheek and using alcohol wipes to remove the sticky residue of duct tape from around my mouth.

I sat, mostly silent, wincing now and then, but mostly staring at the striped wallpaper.

"Are you sure you're okay?" Tommy was bending over, gazing into my eyes. "I'm worried about shock. Are you sure you don't need to go to the hospital?"

"I'm okay." I said the words, but I think I might have been lying. I felt kind of detached, as if I was floating a few inches above myself, looking down at my once again battered body, trying to feel... something. Tommy slipped a blanket over my shoulders, and only then did I realize I was freezing; my teeth were chattering. Where had he gotten the blanket? I hadn't noticed him leave the bathroom... I stared at him, disoriented.

"Come on, Rainie." Tommy took my arm and gently pulled me to my feet. He led me to the living room and sat me on the couch and tucked the blanket in around me.

I closed my eyes against a wave of dizziness.

I opened my eyes again to someone putting a hot cup in my hand. I blinked, for a minute not knowing where I was... Tommy. He was giving me tea. Why?

With a rush it all came back to me, and my heart started thumping painfully again.

Okay, this must be shock, a delayed reaction to my earlier panic. I was okay.

"Rainie?" He brushed my hair back from my face, and as if that gesture had opened a door to somewhere deep inside me I started to cry. Great, wrenching sobs, and in between, words:

"S-so sc-scared! Why? Little dark sp-spaces... tied up... why... "

"I know, Rainie, I know," Tommy had his arms around me, and I was wailing into his shoulder, hysterics coming on. "You're safe now... "

"No! It keeps h-happening... they'll t-take me again... "

"No they won't. It's okay, Rainie, it's okay."

I don't know how long I cried, but eventually I must have fallen asleep, because the next thing I knew I was waking up with a mild headache, my eyes swollen and my sinuses stuffed from the big cry. But otherwise, I felt better.

I looked over at Tommy, who was sitting in a side chair he'd pulled close to the couch so he could hold my hand while I slept. I squeezed his hand gratefully.

"Thank you, Tommy. I feel better."

"I thought you would." He squeezed my hand in return. "Are you hungry?"

"Now that you mention it, I'm starving! But what about Jack and Eddie?"

"Jack texted me a few minutes ago. They know where the other guy is, they're going to collect him."

"Collect him?" I swallowed. "What about the first guy? Did they... I mean, what are they planning to do with them?"

"I don't know, and frankly, I don't care. Do you?"

I stared at Tommy, considering the question. Finally, I answered.

"Yeah, I guess I do. I mean, I don't really advocate killing people, you know?"

"They never said anything about killing them. You worry too much."

Maybe, but I think I was worrying just about enough.

I ate chili and cornbread with Tommy, and then talked him into taking me home. I wanted to check on George and take a hot shower, and most importantly, have my familiar things around me. It seems to me that my claustrophobia should be lightening up a bit, a sort of de-sensitization, but instead each time I find myself bound and confined the panic gets a little worse. As usual, the experience was making me rethink my career choice, but I'm smart enough to understand that's just the fear talking. Once I get my feet back under me I'll probably be right back at it, no holds barred.

"Can you stop at the gas station?" I asked him on the way. "I need a pack of smokes."

"Sure." Tommy didn't know I had quit, and I wasn't going to tell him. This was just a little backslide; I would just smoke a couple, to get over the terror...

George looked no worse for wear after an extra day locked in his cage, although his kibble dish was empty. He eagerly climbed out when I opened his cage, but there was no look of reproach on his face. He just settled under his heat lamp and patiently waited until I brought him fresh food.

I took a shower, but even with Tommy sitting right outside the door I couldn't enjoy it. The bathroom seemed too small, and the water rushing over my face seemed confining, as if it might solidify around me and keep me trapped forever. I washed in a hurry and got out, dressing while I was still damp so I could get the bathroom door open as quickly as possible.

Tommy wanted to hang around, but I convinced him to go on home. Jack and Eddie had the bad guys under control, and I just wanted to be alone for awhile to lick my wounds in private. I was embarrassed by my breakdown; it seemed so... *girly*.

It was nearly dark by the time I got a text from Jack: "*on our way.*" I went out to sit on the porch to smoke while I waited, eager to know just exactly what he and Eddie had done with my kidnappers.

Eddie's Charger pulled into the driveway behind my Escort, and both men got out. They looked tired but unharmed.

"You okay?" Eddie asked me.

"Sure. Are you?"

He grinned. "Never better."

I looked at Jack, and his eyes met mine. With a shock, I realized I hadn't given a thought to the fact that we'd shared a bed. I had forgotten all about my concerns over our new status. Was he still planning to dump me? Would he give me an update on my kidnappers and then a casual brush off? Or was he really my boyfriend now?

I felt my face flush, and Jack gave me a slow smile.

"Hey." He pulled me into his arms and held tight for a minute. He kissed me on the forehead and let me go. Damn, that didn't tell me much, did it?

"Let's go inside," Eddie suggested. I nodded dumbly and led the way into the house.

"So?" We were sitting in the living room, each with a beer. "What did you do to them? Who were they?" I realized I referred to them in past tense; I was fairly certain they were no longer among the living. But Eddie surprised me.

"We sent them to South American with some mutual friends."

"Really?"

"They have some prison time coming. I can't guarantee their continued health, but they were still breathing when we turned them over."

I just looked at him, skeptical.

"Hey, give us some credit, Rainie," Jack complained. "We knew how you'd feel about an outright execution."

"Okay," I nodded, deciding to believe them.

"They were brothers, Gary and Greg Cavanaugh, free lance mercenaries."

"They were part of our group, hired to help the latest despot assert control," Eddie explained. "The despot wasn't a great guy or anything, but he was better than some. He definitely didn't approve of burning women and children to death."

"So, these were the guys who burned the school, right? Killed seven kids?" Jack had told me this story before.

"And their teacher. Actually, Gary set the fire, claiming the teacher was defying the new order. I caught up to him a few months later and turned him over to the authorities down there."

"Really? I'm surprised you didn't mete out your own justice."

"Damn, Rainie, do you think I just go around killing every bad guy I run into?"

I just looked at him.

"Okay, so in this case I wanted to make a point. We were in the midst of some rather delegate negotiations with the despot in control, and we needed to prove we were on his side.

"So I turned Cavanaugh over and he was convicted and set for execution, but he escaped. Thing is, South American prisons aren't much concerned with prisoner's rights; he lost an eye and a kidney before he managed to get out. He figured that was my fault."

I vaguely remembered the patch on the guy's eye, and my little voice making pirate jokes. It almost made me smile, but I stayed on topic.

"Just because you arrested him?"

"Well, mostly." Jack shrugged. "We had a couple of run-ins before that, when we were supposedly fighting on the same side. He's a bad guy, Rainie, a cancer. The world would be a better place with him cut out of it."

"But you didn't 'cut him out.'"

"No, I didn't."

"But not because he didn't deserve it," Eddie added. He smiled. "I think Jack's going soft; he's hanging around you too much."

I rolled my eyes. "Yeah, soft and cuddly, that's Jack for you."

"Anyway, we turned the brothers over to a couple of mercenaries that share a history with them. They'll take them down to South America to face the original charges."

"But I thought that was just for Gary; what about his brother?"

Jack shrugged. "I'm sure they'll think of something."

"So this isn't at all a legal solution, is it? You just turned them over to someone else to do your dirty work."

"What do you think we should have done? Slapped their noses with newspapers and told them 'no! bad boys!'?"

"Of course not!" I shook my head, remembering my own violent fantasies, and how badly I hoped Jack would tear those guys limb from limb. I sighed. "Actually, I guess I admire your restraint."

Eddie smiled and yawned. "Look, I drove in from Chicago to help with this little project; I've been up thirty-six straight hours. I need to get some sleep." He stood up and looked at Jack.

"I think I'll hang around awhile." He glanced over at me. "You mind giving me a ride home later?"

"Um, no... sure, that's okay." But was it? I was already so emotionally drained, I didn't know if I was ready for alone time with Jack. I got up to walk Eddie to the door.

Eddie looked from me to Jack, and shook his head. He muttered something under his breath that sounded suspiciously like a swear word. He stopped halfway out the door and turned back to me.

"You be careful, okay?"

"Hey, I'm safe now. You got all the bad guys."

Eddie looked past my shoulder at Jack and frowned. "Not all of them, Rainie." He hugged me and walked to his car. Well, what the hell did that mean? He'd warned me about Jack before, but he'd never said he was a bad guy. Did I really have something to worry about here?

I closed the door. Jack was standing there, staring at me intently.

"It's been a rough couple of days, hasn't it?"

"That's a bit of an understatement."

"I'm hoping it's just the trauma you've been through that has you looking at me like I might be an axe murderer or a child killer."

"I am still a little on edge."

Jack nodded. "So maybe not a good time to talk about the other night?"

I flushed at the memory. "Maybe not."

"Okay, no talking." He held out his hand, and I took it, I admit, a bit hesitantly. He pulled me down to sit next to him on the couch and put his arms around me. For a while we sat there like that, me stiff as a board, worried about his intentions. But he just kept holding me, and I eventually relaxed; it did feel pretty good.

"Wait!" I sat up abruptly. "What about Smitty? And Riley..."

"Belinda bailed Smitty out," Jack pulled me back into his arms. "And Riley's situation can wait until tomorrow."

He was right, of course.

I slumped against him, my head on his

shoulder, and he lightly ran his fingers up and down my arm. True to his word, he didn't talk.

Sooner or later, I suppose we'll have to figure out our relationship. Or if we really even have one.

But for now, I would take the silence, and the strong arms... and I fell asleep.

Made in the USA
Middletown, DE
06 November 2014